BATHING BEAUTY

From where Gavin stood he faced the kitchen, a small one-person affair. To his right was the living room, perhaps twelve by twelve. A short hall led from the living room to the bedroom, the door to which stood open.

Off the hall was the bathroom.

Gavin heard a noise. A low, indistinct sort of noise, perhaps a shower curtain settling into place, perhaps caused by the draft from an open window, perhaps nothing more than the crankings of Gavin's supercharged imagination.

Gavin crossed the living room silently. He reached under his left arm and pulled out the Walther P-38. Its weight felt comforting in his hand. When he reached the bathroom door he stopped, listening.

Nothing.

He entered the bathroom quickly, crossing the small room in two steps. His hand gripped the plastic flower-pattern shower curtain and he tore it open.

She was beautiful. She stood in the bathtub, fully clothed.

Her eyes were round with fear, her red, full-lipped mouth open in breathless anticipation. Gavin realized he was pointing the P-38 between her full, upswept breasts.

"Hi," Gavin said.

"Don't shoot," she whispered.

Gavin slid the P-38 into its holster. "Wouldn't think of it," he said. "Not on the first date, anyway."

The Terminator Series

#1: MERCENARY KILL

the TERMINATOR #2

SILICON VALLEY SLAUGHTER

by John Quinn

PINNACLE BOOKS NEW YORK

This is a work of fiction. All the characters and events portrayed in this book are fictional, and any resemblance to real people or incidents is purely coincidental.

THE TERMINATOR #2:
SILICON VALLEY SLAUGHTER

An original Pinnacle Books edition, published for the first time anywhere.

First printing, July 1983

ISBN: 0-523-42043-9

Cover illustration by Bruce Minney

Printed in the United States of America

PINNACLE BOOKS, INC.
1430 Broadway
New York, New York 10018

SILICON VALLEY SLAUGHTER

prologue—the icebreaker

Thomas Scanlon took U.S. 101 north, leaving San Jose at three-thirty in the afternoon. The southbound lanes of 101 were already crowded with commuters returning home from San Francisco, Scanlon's destination. Scanlon knew the type well enough, the clowns who worked in San Francisco and then made the haul home every night, ties loose around their necks, their tongues hanging out for that before-dinner martini.

Their workday was already over. Thomas Scanlon's had just begun.

His decision to drive to San Francisco had been a spur-of-the-moment thing, but that was the kind of guy that Scanlon was: No Pussyfooting Allowed. Those damned Japs didn't want to do their part of the deal unless they could do it in the dark, with no one to see them. But Susan Billings was under constant surveillance, and the Japs whined that they didn't know what the hell to do about it.

Scanlon did. He told Shigata to do it at seven o'clock, and the place would be clear. It was like having to deal with babies, for chrissakes!

Scanlon was mad. So what if the broad was under surveillance? Scanlon would take care of it if those nutless wonders didn't want to. He patted the soft leather case on the seat beside him. He could feel the hard cold mass of the .44 Magnum. It gave him comfort.

Scanlon glanced in the rearview mirror, his wide-set blue eyes innocent and clear. His thick red hair, barely long enough to part, grew low on his temples and gave him a youthful look. But he was forty-five years old and still damned near broke.

He exited 101 just before the Civic Center and wound up on Fillmore Street heading north. He didn't visit San Francisco that often: so he took time to get his bearings. Scanlon was on familiar ground only in North Beach, San Francisco's sexual free-fire zone. Topless dancers had given way to live sex shows, twenty-four-hour-a-day porno movie theaters, transvestite/transsexual nightclubs, and hard-core crazies of every type. Scanlon enjoyed its atmosphere. He felt right at home.

Scanlon turned right and crossed Van Ness

Avenue. He smiled. Van Ness—now he knew where he was. He drove east to the Columbus Avenue intersection. Took that to Bay Street. He parked near the intersection.

Thick fog was rolling in. Scanlon walked now. Over his gray suit he wore a London Fog raincoat that had been draped over the passenger's seat. The misty chill put him in a good mood. The cool wet air was fresh on his face, a tonic, easing the tension he felt around his eyes and mouth.

Good killing weather.

He felt the .44 in the pocket of his raincoat as he walked half a block west on Bay Street. The fog was thicker now; Bay Street, quiet and clean.

Scanlon entered a three-story building and took the stairs to the second floor. He felt calm, at ease, a man who had already decided on a course of action and now had but to carry it out.

He knocked on the heavy black wood door, his right hand gripped around the .44, now out of his pocket and held under the front fold of his raincoat.

The man that opened the door had a chicken drumstick in his hand and grease smeared on his lips. "Yeah?" His brown hair was blow-dried. His turtleneck sweater was stale with cigarette smoke. "What can I do for you?"

Scanlon waved him back inside the apartment with the .44. His eyes grew large and round when he saw the steel in Scanlon's hand. "Jesus," he said. "Don't get nervous, man. Just don't get nervous."

Scanlon took in the arrangement quickly. Standard surveillance deal. No furniture except for the table and chair and cot, but about twenty thousand dollars' worth of electronics. All those damned little lights made Scanlon mad. Damn computers are going to ruin us all.

"Let's go," Scanlon said.

"Go?"

"Let's go," Scanlon said again.

"Look—this is just business. You want to steal something, go ahead and steal it. I don't give a shit. It's all government money, man. Take it all."

Scanlon went to single action and the man went white around the eyes. "Ok, chief," he said. "Don't get fucking nervous is all."

They walked back to the Buick and Scanlon let him get in, then slid in beside him. "Drive to Marin," Scanlon said. "Let's see how the white people live."

They took the Golden Gate Bridge and Scanlon let him do all the talking. Scanlon wasn't listening. There wasn't any point to it. He told Scanlon about his family, and there was a baby on the way, and all the rest of it, but Scanlon had heard those stories before, and they didn't impress him one way or the other.

The guy had a dangerous occupation. If he was so damned worried about his family he should've found something safer to do for a living.

By the time they took the coast road cutoff the driver was sweating. Scanlon had to admit to himself that he enjoyed all the discomfort he was causing. Scanlon liked to see men crawl and cry before they died.

He had the younger man take the Stinson Beach road and finally told him to pull over near a stand of tall trees. The road was deserted and the fog, thick and cold. Scanlon took the bolt cutter and a Hefty bag from the trunk.

Scanlon walked him into the woods and when he turned around to make a final plea Scanlon squeezed one round directly into his face. His skull exploded and the long hair framing his ears caught fire. Scanlon pumped one more round into the jaw, destroying any chances of identification through dental records.

The bolt cutter took care of the dead man's fingers, which Scanlon carefully deposited in the Hefty bag. When he was finished, Scanlon looked down at the remains. Good job.

one

High Card, Colorado

"Ratatattat!"

Gavin froze. He had just entered Dorn's office as the burly bearded mechanic whirled around. Dorn held an Uzi submachine gun in his hands. It was pointed at Gavin.

"Ratatattat!" Dorn chattered, a big grin on his face.

"Point that damned thing somewhere else," Gavin said.

"It's not loaded, you know. What kind of an asshole do you think I am anyway?"

Gavin held out his hand and Dorn handed the Uzi to him. Gavin checked it over. Clean, almost new. "Nice one," Gavin said, handing it back. "Where'd you get it?"

"A gun show over in Denver. I'd never been to one before. They sell the damned things right out in the open. More stuff than you can imagine, or at least more than I could imagine." He shook his head. "I had no idea of the kinds of weapons you could just go out and buy."

"What the hell are you going to do with it? You don't like guns."

Dorn slapped the Uzi's short barrel. "Nice piece of machined metal. That's all I saw. I took one look and fell in love with the damned thing. Don't even know how to use it!"

The sight and feel of the Uzi had stirred dark memories in Gavin. He lit a cigarette, depositing the match in the jar lid that served as Dorn's desk ashtray. He waited while Dorn put away the Uzi. "I'm heading over towards Denver," Gavin finally said. "There's an auction that might have what I need."

Dorn nodded. "You do that. I'll hang around till I hear from you. Nothing later than a '75—a '74 would be best."

"OK," Gavin said. He was wearing a blue down parka, Levi's, and a pair of low-heel Frye boots. "And don't play around with that Uzi. Those things can get ugly fast."

"I told you," Dorn said, "that the damned thing isn't even loaded!"

San Francisco

The meeting with special agents Kelly and Rogers had been dull but necessary. Duffy never enjoyed dealing with field men—they viewed him with suspicion, as a member of the fuddleheaded Washington bureaucracy, the paper-shufflers who didn't know how to get out of their own way. FBI personnel were rarely pleasant, Duffy thought. They brought their own special brand of Official Paranoia to any meeting with an outsider. Even though Duffy was a Justice Department official, that wasn't quite inside enough, as far as Kelly and Rogers were concerned.

The meeting had been held in Duffy's room at the St. Francis, on Union Square. Room service had delivered a pot of coffee and service for three; the agents had presented their reports, refused a cup of coffee, then sat primly while Duffy scanned the paperwork. Outside the window a gray San Francisco fog stirred. Duffy wanted to get rid of Kelly and Rogers as quickly as possible.

It was Duffy's last night in San Francisco. He wasn't going to spend it in a cramped hotel room with two guys who buffed their brogans on the backs of their pants.

Duffy removed his glasses and laid them on the nightstand. "Looks good," he said. "I'll go over it more thoroughly in the morning."

Special Agent Rogers cleared his throat. "We expected a decision this evening," he said.

Duffy chuckled. "Now you boys must know that a quick decision is something that never happens in a situation like this." He watched the two agents exchange Significant Glances. Duffy decided to rub it in. "I've got to report to the executive committee. They'll take a meeting or two and then submit a report to the second assistant to the Attorney General. The A.G.'s appointments secretary will schedule a meeting, and then we'll have a round or two of informal hearings."

"I guess we'll be going," Special Agent Kelly said as he stood up.

"Sure you wouldn't like a cup of coffee? Damned fine stuff, I can assure you."

"Thanks. We'll await word from Washington, then?"

Duffy walked them to the door. "Fellows, the report looks all right to me. Maybe a question or two about the expenses. I wouldn't give it another thought." Duffy certainly wasn't going to.

As soon as they were gone Duffy tossed the report into his briefcase, mixed a J & B with tap water, and reclined on the bed, sipping his whiskey as he watched the fog move outside his window.

It was only six o'clock, so Duffy decided to shower and shave, then head downstairs for a fine dinner in the hotel's dining room. Most hotel restaurants didn't merit a visit, but Duffy had always enjoyed this one.

Just as he finished his whiskey and water he remembered Susan.

Damn! He had told Marianne that he would visit Susan, see how she was doing. Susan was Marianne's favorite niece, a beautiful girl with an I.Q. of 170. Susan often made Duffy uncomfortable.

Since Susan had moved out west, in defiance of the family's advice, Marianne had been worried sick. No matter how much Duffy told Marianne that California was actually just another state in the Union, that people there wore shoes, she refused to admit that civilized life was possible west of the Mississippi. Susan was bound to come to no good.

So when Marianne heard that Duffy was headed west on department business she had extracted a promise from him that he would visit Susan. See how she was doing.

Damn!

If it wasn't for the fact that Marianne had the good sense and the even better good taste to prefer Duffy to a host of other men, he wouldn't bother. But he'd made an ass of himself the last time he'd seen Marianne, and he didn't want to botch this one.

Duffy crossed the room to his briefcase parked on the desk under the mirror. He fished out his address book, located Susan

Billings' phone number, then finished his drink.

Duffy dialed the number.

"Hello?"

"Hi there," Duffy said. "This is Jack Duffy, from D.C. How are you?"

"Fine, Jack. Are you in San Francisco?"

"Sure am. Just here for the night, though. I thought maybe I could take you to dinner. Sound all right with you?"

There was a pause. "I've got this work . . . but to hell with it! I'd love to! I've been penned up in the apartment for over a week, and I need a break!"

"Well, that's great," Duffy said. He told Susan he'd be there around seven, if that was all right. "Don't want to rush you," he said.

"That's perfect," she said. "I can be ready in ten minutes if I have to."

Duffy had heard that before.

Duffy showered, shaved, was dressed before six-thirty. He picked up his battered trench-coat, stuffed Susan's address in the pocket, and went downstairs.

It was a wonderful San Francisco night, cool and misty, the streets shrouded and mysterious. Duffy climbed in a hotel cab and settled back for an interesting ride.

It was dark by the time the tow truck arrived at Dorn's garage just off Main Street.

Gavin hopped down from the passenger's side, then told the driver to hold on for a moment. Dorn had said he'd keep the place open till Gavin got there, but the sliding door was down at the garage entrance. Gavin hoped that Dorn hadn't forgotten.

He banged on the office door and was relieved to see a light come on. Dorn opened the door, wiping his hands on an orange shop rag. He'd been working in the garage and had walked through the darkened office to answer the door. The light had come from the work floor of the garage, which was connected to the office by an interior door.

"What in hell took so long?" Dorn asked. "I was about to head outta here."

"Glad you waited," Gavin said. The tow truck driver sounded his horn and Dorn yelled for him to hold his horses.

"I'll go get the garage door," Dorn said to Gavin. "You tell that asshole to pull 'er right in."

Dorn had cleared a space on the right-hand side of his work floor; it took the truck driver about two minutes to wheel in, release his cargo, then pull out, a job well done. When the tow truck was gone, Dorn and Gavin stood in silent appreciation of what it had delivered.

"Looks like a real piece of shit," Dorn said.

Gavin walked around it, kicking the tires.

"Three hundred and fifty dollars. I kind of like it."

The object of their remarks was a 1974 Pontiac Trans Am, a Super Duty 455. It was black, the body in good shape. Dorn had opened the hood and was considering the engine. "You're real lucky you know me," he said to Gavin.

Dorn's work was restoring classic automobiles. He specialized in Bugattis. There were four of them in the shop needing various parts and services, all of which Dorn would get to in his own sweet time. Auto restoration was a lucrative field for a man as good with his hands as Dorn. But all the money that he made went for the pleasures of life, of which Dorn had sampled—and become addicted to—quite a few.

Gavin rubbed his hand over his chin, feeling the day's growth of beard. He felt dirty and tired as he looked at the sludge-covered engine of the Trans Am. A crisp cool breeze brought the scent of late fall through the garage's open door, a clean smell of leaves, campfires, sudden high-mountain snows.

Gavin suddenly thought about Kendall, remembering what had gone wrong.

Dorn slammed the hood and grinned at him. "You did good," Dorn said. "Just like I said. I'm surprised they had an old Trans

Am ready to go. Police auctions rarely have what you want."

"But the engine's shot and the tires are gone," Gavin said. "How the hell are we going to make this car go?"

Dorn was wiping his hands on his back-pocket rag again. "You ever hear of Arnie 'the Farmer' Beswick?" Dorn asked.

The cab pulled up outside a three-story apartment building on Bay Street between Columbus and Van Ness. Duffy handed the driver ten dollars and told him to wait.

There was no doorman or any other kind of security that Duffy could see. He took the stairs to the third floor, and his wheezing breath made him realize just how out of shape he was. Apartment 3-D was at the end of the hall. Duffy knocked, and the door gave under his hand.

He pushed in and froze. Susan Billings was being restrained by an Oriental who had one hand around her waist, the other over her mouth. She was struggling, her eyes wild, but she was no match for the short, wiry young man who held her.

Duffy started forward—he saw out of the corner of his eye that the Oriental was not alone. There were two others, stocky, block-faced men, standing just to the right of the door.

They came at him without a word and Duffy turned to meet them. He remembered enough of his college boxing days to balance himself before throwing the first punch. It landed flush on the jaw of the one coming in, but Duffy's balance wasn't what it used to be. The force of the punch carried Duffy around. Before he could regain his footing he felt something cold and hard alongside his head. While there was no pain, he was aware that he had been clubbed with a .45 automatic, because he could see it in the other guy's hand.

He was on the floor, the room spinning. There was a wetness on his neck, bile rising from his stomach. He tried to get up and the one with the .45 stepped in and hit him again. Before everything went black Duffy saw the automatic coming down a final time.

The cab driver waited for forty-five minutes before he decided to check on his passenger. The only reason he waited forty-five minutes was because he'd smoked a joint of seedless and had lost track of the time. He found Duffy on the carpet just inside the apartment on the third floor. He saw that Duffy was still breathing, then called the cops.

Inspector Dan Cooke had been called in

when the first cops on the scene found Duffy's I.D. and saw that he was Justice Department. Cooke was on the scene fifteen minutes later, arriving simultaneously with the ambulance team. "What have we got?" he asked a detective on the investigative unit.

"Apartment's leased to Susan Billings. She's gone, no one knows when to expect her. Cabbie dropped off Duffy and was told to wait. When nothing happened, he decided to check it out. Found him on the floor." Cooke nodded. He turned to the cabbie.

"He tell you anything in the cab? Say anything about what he was up to?"

The cabbie swallowed and tried to remember. "Just told me to step on it," he said. "The guy was real anxious to get here."

Inspector Dan Cooke shook his head. "Looks like he made it," Cooke said.

Three hours later Inspector Cooke was at the North Beach Station wondering how to handle it. First off: Jack Duffy was a single man, and in San Francisco, *single* is synonymous with *gay*. Was this just another twisted chapter in the never-ending saga of middle-aged men trading rough? To make matters worse, the guy was Justice Department, in from Washington. Cooke knew how sensitive the Feds could get when the term *gay* was bandied about.

On the other hand, there was an excellent chance the guy wasn't gay. After all, the apartment belonged to a woman named Susan Billings.

Initial word on Susan Billings was that she was an employee of Electrotec down in San Jose. She worked out of the San Francisco office, had no record, and drove an '80 Porsche 914, which was still parked in the apartment building's garage.

The word from the hospital was that Duffy was in a coma. They really didn't know what the hell was going to happen to him.

Cooke put out a general bulletin over the wire to Washington, Chicago, and New York. Maybe he'd get lucky.

After all, the guy *is* Justice Department. Might as well touch all the bases.

two

It was a bright clear day chilled by a fall wind from the north. Gavin wore a white wool sweater, jeans, and running shoes. It only took ten minutes to walk down from his hillside cabin to High Card's Main Street, then two blocks down and around the corner to Dorn's.

The big double door was open and Dorn was tinkering with the upright engine of a Bugatti roadster. Gavin thought it was a 1931, but he wasn't sure, and he didn't want to ask. Any question about a Bugatti was likely to set Dorn off on a rambling account that would contain More Than Anyone Ever Wanted To Know About Bugattis.

"Any coffee around?" Gavin asked. Dorn pointed to the office without looking up and Gavin went in and poured thick dark liquid into a cup.

He took a sip. Maybe it was coffee after all. He wasn't sure.

He walked back to the shop area, put down his cup on the hood of the Trans Am, and lit a cigarette. Dorn stood up, stretched, shook his head. "Checked it out this morning," he said to Gavin. "All systems are go."

Gavin smiled. "So it was a good buy after all?"

"I told you," Dorn said. "I've got the stuff to make this car a wonderful deal."

"I don't want to spend a lot," Gavin said. He had a little over twenty-two thousand dollars in his stash, but he had no money coming in. He needed a car, but he didn't want to spend a lot of money. Dorn had told him to pick up an old Trans Am. If possible, Dorn would fix it up for him.

"I already got the engine," Dorn said. "Damned good one too. You ever hear of—"

"Arnie 'the Farmer' Beswick," Gavin said, shaking his head. "No. I never have. So what?"

Dorn walked to the workbench beside the Trans Am and tugged the cloth from a sizable object concealed beneath it. Gavin walked over to check the V-8 engine—clean and powerful. "Nice," he said. "Looks a little big for the Trans Am."

"It'll work," Dorn said. "It was built for Arnie's Grocery Wagon in '63. Arnie was hot then. Best Pontiac race driver I ever saw." Dorn tapped the engine. "NASCAR quality. Better than you deserve."

"What's my speed with that thing stuck in the Trans Am?"

Dorn narrowed his eyes and made some mental calculations. " 'Course, I'm figuring new wheels and tires too—specials, sixteen-inch wheels and Pirelli P-7's . . ."

"The jargon's wasted on me. How fast will it go?"

"Plus the Airesearch turbocharger I got on the trade with that trucker . . ."

"How fast?"

"One hundred fifty miles an hour. I'd advise you to install four Koni shocks too."

"Anything else?"

Dorn pointed to the hood of the Trans Am, on which was the pinstripe rendition of the Trans Am logo, an eagle with outstretched wings.

"Get it painted," Dorn said, "and tell them to leave off the Screaming Chicken."

Inspector Dan Cooke crushed out his cigarette in the metal ashtray by the elevator. The white hospital corridor was empty, save for the few people gathered around the nurse's station midway down the hall.

When Cooke saw Dr. Brandt come out of Duffy's room he walked down the hall, intercepting the gray-haired physician before he could dart into the lounge.

"Ah, Inspector Cooke. Still on the job?" Dr. Brandt checked his Rolex. "Pretty late. I assume Mr. Duffy is a VIP. Not the usual thing, you know. Having an inspector on the premises like this."

Cooke nodded. "How is he? Any improvement? Did he say anything?"

Brandt shook his head. "He hasn't been conscious since he was brought in," Brandt said. "Frankly—perhaps I'm overly pessimistic—I don't think there's much hope. He was traumatized quite severely. Pistol-whipped, I'd say, or beaten with some sort of metal instrument. It's a wonder he's alive."

"What can we expect?"

"Unless he comes out of it soon, I'm afraid the prognosis will be even less optimistic. He's not in the best of shape—overweight, poor muscle tone, all of that. Slightly anemic. Blood pressure's no good at all. It all adds up in the face of an injury like that."

Cooke nodded. This wasn't good, not good at all. Word from Washington was that Duffy was in San Francisco on official department business. Apparently he wasn't gay—Susan Billings had turned out to be the niece of Duffy's fiancée in Washington. The Billings family had a lot of juice in the Nation's

Capital. There had already been two calls from the commissioner.

Tomorrow it would be worse. When politics mixes in with police work it can get nasty fast. It can also get dangerous to a policeman's career fast. Cooke wanted to make sure he wasn't missing a trick. He thanked Dr. Brandt, then left the hospital.

His stomach was churning. Cooke thought about picking up a bottle of Maalox. Instead, he ducked into the first bar he saw on Brannan Street and ordered a double Scotch.

It wasn't bad enough that his daughter was pregnant. Or that the father-to-be didn't want to get married because he was still not sure that marriage was a viable institution.

Now Cooke had the commissioner in his ear, telling him that the Duffy matter was not something that could be filed and forgotten. Cooke sipped his whiskey and reviewed what he had.

Jack Duffy comes to San Francisco on a swing through the western states, touching bases with the local FBI offices. He picks up reports, pats everyone on the ass, and finally gets to San Francisco, his last stop.

He meets with two agents named Kelly and Rogers in his hotel room. He doesn't tell them he plans to go out that evening. As soon as they leave—or within thirty minutes—he takes a cab and goes to the apartment of Susan Billings. There is a record of a phone call from his hotel room to the Billings apartment.

And then—*nada*.

The cabbie didn't see a thing. Didn't see anyone leave, didn't see anyone go in. When the cabbie checked to see where his passenger had gone, he finds Duffy in a pool of his own blood just inside Susan Billings's apartment.

Inspector Dan Cooke ordered another double Scotch and decided he'd call in and sign off. He wasn't going to get a damned thing done anyway. Maybe something would break in the morning. Maybe he'd get assigned to another case. Maybe Duffy would recover and confess that he did it to himself.

New York City

Nick Coletti didn't know Inspector Dan Cooke of the SFPD, but if he had, he would have identified with his fellow cop's glum conclusions. Sometimes being a cop wasn't all it was cracked up to be.

Coletti was working overtime and not liking it a bit. He'd gotten up to get another cup of coffee and had decided to check the wire, more out of curiosity than anything else. He was in the final stages of his twenty years with the New York Police Department;

the whole thing boiled down to: Don't fuck up the pension.

Coletti read Cooke's wire bulletin on Duffy while he sipped his hot coffee. Duffy was Gavin's friend, of that Coletti was positive. How many Jack Duffys could there be at the Justice Department?

Gavin was still in Colorado—or had been the last time Coletti had been in touch with him. Gavin wouldn't have a clue about what had happened to his buddy Duffy. Maybe he'd better get word to Gavin about Duffy. Gavin would like to know—he and Duffy had gotten pretty tight.

Nick Coletti glanced up as Detective Bill Alexander started interviewing a witness. Coletti yawned, the repetition of the questioning making him sleepy.

Of the twenty desks in Coletti's squad room, over half were empty. Alexander was the only cop with a live one present. Coletti returned to his desk and carefully set down the cup of coffee. Too many ruined reports, too much dripping paperwork had instilled in him a careful regard for the potential damage contained in an innocent-looking cup of coffee.

Coletti had known Gavin since both men served in Vietnam. After the war Coletti had joined an organization, the NYPD; Gavin had joined an organization too. Only Gavin's was shadowy, secret, lethal. Coletti knew that much, but not much more.

Gavin was out of it now. He was still living in High Card, Colorado, as far as Coletti knew. When Gavin was still working for the spook agency, Coletti had been the only man alive who knew how to reach Gavin directly. Every Monday Coletti would buy a copy of the *Wall Street Journal,* and if a certain ad was running in the classifieds, he would know that Gavin was being summoned for a job. That was the agency's only method of contacting Gavin, who had built up a new identity in the tiny Colorado town. There, Gavin was known as Bob Evans.

The guy might even be married by now, Coletti thought. Maybe he didn't want to know about any of this. What could he do about it anyway? His buddy, Duffy, was already hurt. Maybe he ought to just file the report from San Francisco and forget about it.

Coletti inhaled deeply on his cigarette, a low-tar-and-nicotine number that his Stop-Smoking Program had recommended. He was smoking twice as many of the damned things as his old brand.

He hadn't seen Gavin in months—maybe a year, for chrissakes. Time was getting away from Coletti. He ground out his cigarette, finished the cup of coffee. It was quiet in the precinct. Coletti was exhausted.

Gavin was no longer doing whatever it was he used to do. If he brought him into this Duffy thing, was he doing Gavin a favor or not? Maybe Gavin wants to stay uninvolved. Gavin had done his share; maybe he'd rather someone else did it for a change.

It was no use. Coletti couldn't make Gavin's decision for him.

Coletti composed the message to Gavin, then slid the paper into the time slot, clocked it, and hand-carried it downstairs to Communications.

Jimmy Shigata walked down Commercial Street, a narrow avenue just off San Francisco's main Chinatown thoroughfares. He had eaten lunch at the diner on the corner of Grant Avenue, a pepper beef sandwich and a side of fries. Now, walking back to the warehouse, his hands thrust into his pants pockets, he felt better prepared to deal with his problems, which were compounding by the minute.

Shigata wore Jordache jeans, Puma running shoes, and a pullover cashmere sweater that hugged his slender figure. He was twenty-seven years old, but looked fifteen to Caucasian eyes. While those same Caucasian eyes would merely note the passage of a casually dressed Chinese youth, oriental eyes would know better. Shigata was of Japanese descent, a third-generation American, not totally at ease in San Francisco's Chinatown.

But that was the least of his problems.

What had started out as a simple operation had taken a sour turn: Who was to know that the guy they cold-cocked was from the Justice Department?

Shigata swore under his breath and shook his head as he headed toward the street-front warehouse in the middle of the block. They were going to have to ride it out and that wasn't in the plan. The plan had been to take the girl directly to Los Angeles and hold her there while they arranged passage to Japan. There, she would service any man that they wanted her to. When they were through with her, Susan Billings would be junk.

But now, with all the heat, moving her was out of the question. Especially when Shigata considered the men he was working with. Why they wouldn't let him use guys from Little Tokyo, in Los Angeles, was beyond him. Shigata needed men who spoke English and knew their way around. But the *Yakuza* he was stuck with couldn't speak English, looked like villains in a James Bond movie, and thought eating raw fish was a wonderful deal.

No one would listen to him. Shigata had argued, explaining that he would be more comfortable with guys he had worked with before. But no one cared. The men Shigata was forced to work with had been imported from Japan, *yakuza,* enforcers from the Japanese Mafia.

Mr. Oki had explained to Shigata, as if he were an uninformed *putz* from the San Fernando Valley, that the *yakuza* were highly respected in the old country, known for their many charitable works. They were men of honor who *belonged.* They were members of a society that took care of them as long as they were loyal and true to their society.

But it wasn't like working for Toyota. If a *yakuza* screwed up, his masters punished him by cutting off his pinky finger. There were a lot of *yakuza* with only three fingers, and Shigata had four of them in the warehouse, talking guttural Japanese to each other, looking at Shigata as if he were some sort of mutant.

Part of it was the language. Shigata's Japanese was bad, but it was good enough to get things done. But his inability to speak fluently constituted a loss of face that was difficult to deal with.

The *yakuza* all wore gray suits, carefully tailored; they looked like stocky, cold-eyed businessmen. Shigata dressed in a more casual style; that didn't sit well either.

And now he was penned up with those four kamikazes until it was safe to move.

All that, and a football strike too. It just wasn't fair.

Jimmy Shigata used the larger key on the dead bolt and the smaller one on the door lock. Once inside, he put the keys on the shelf by the boarded-over window and threw the dead bolt home.

The phone was ringing when he entered the large room, lit by a single overhead bulb. Against the far wall, tied spread-eagle to the bedframe, Susan Billings watched him intently. There was fear in her eyes. Her mouth was covered with a wide strip of adhesive.

The four *yakuza* were staring at Shigata, silently ordering him to answer the phone.

It was a wall phone and Shigata snatched the receiver off the hook, cradling it between his ear and shoulder. He used his hands to pull out a cigarette and light it.

"Hello?"

"We have a problem," the deep steady voice said. "A serious problem." Shigata recognized Mr. Oki's precise choice of words.

"Don't blame me," Shigata said, shifting the receiver into his hand. "Accidents happen."

"Don't talk to me about accidents," the

voice said. "The man you assaulted might recover. Have you thought about that?"

"So?"

"So we are not prepared for that eventuality. It would have been simpler to kill him on the spot, but you neglected to do that. Now there is a witness who merely has to regain consciousness."

Shigata felt cold droplets of perspiration trail down his rib cage. "You want us to go into the hospital and off him right there?"

"I think that action is indicated."

"How?"

There was a deep laughter on the other end of the line. "You can do it any way you want. You can hold a pillow over his face or inject an air bubble in an artery or dismember him with a steak knife. How it is done is immaterial to us. But you must do it, and quickly." The line went dead. Shigata held the receiver to his ear for a moment longer, the dial tone making him feel foolish.

The Japan-America Trading Corporation was headquartered on Los Angeles' Miracle Mile—Wilshire Boulevard, the high-rise commercial center of Souther California. With offices in the California Federal Building across from the world-famous La Brea Tar Pits, the Japan-America Trading Corporation was known mainly for its lobbying efforts in American political circles, efforts aimed at increasing the already favorable Japanese balance of trade with the United States.

In reality, the Japan-America Trading Corporation was not an official, or unofficial, representative of the Japanese Government in any manner whatsoever. It was an arm of Japanese intelligence, and its main purpose was to keep abreast of developments in American technology.

From his ninth-floor office, Hirofumi Oki had an excellent view of the Hollywood Hills, the entertainment district known as Sunset Strip, which lies below the hills, and the tall white building near the Veteran's Cemetery in Westwood that housed the local offices of the Central Intelligence Agency.

He was known simply as Mr. Oki. An elegantly dressed, prosperous-looking man, Mr. Oki never revealed anything by the expression on his face. When things were going well, or when things were going badly, Mr. Oki's expression never changed.

Today, things were going badly. Mr. Oki sat in his high-back executive swivel chair and considered his options.

Simply put, his options had narrowed down to one: the successful acquisition of the encryption device plans. With such a success, he would once again find favor with his superiors, a committee of political-industrial leaders in Tokyo.

His last venture had turned into an unmitigated disaster on several levels.

The *yakuza,* with whom he worked closely, had demanded a shipment of arms—something that is very difficult, given the laws in Japan and the incorruptibility of its customs agents. Mr. Oki had pondered the problem for weeks, and had finally hit upon a solution that he considered brilliant.

A Buddhist monk, a complete innocent, had been recruited in Japan to conduct a mission of national honor. The monk was to travel to Saipan, where one of the bloodiest battles of World War II had been fought. There, the monk would recover the bodies of valiant Japanese soldiers, and escort the remains to Japan for a belated, and thoroughly honorable, burial.

The arms, already shipped to Saipan, were hidden among the remains of Japan's valiant soldiers. Once in Japan, the arms were to be recovered by the *yakuza.*

An alert customs agent—who, Oki reasoned, must have been a necrophiliac—had discovered the weapons, bringing great dishonor upon the *yakuza* involved. The Yakuza were not pleased, nor were Mr. Oki's superiors. The plans for the device would set matters right. But Oki could afford no more mistakes.

A thin smile straightened Oki's lips. He would not allow the operation to be compromised by those in the offices of the Japan-America Trading Corporation who would gleefully obstruct Oki's plan if allowed to. The corporation was filled with ambitious men, and by pushing Oki aside, their own advancement would be made easier.

Oki concluded that the operation would be carried out in his private rooms atop the Lotus Restaurant, in Little Tokyo, the Japanese section of downtown Los Angeles.

Oki picked up the telephone. He would have to order computers installed—computers of sufficient sophistication to verify the plans that would be contained on the microcassette. Those plans, when they reached their final destination, would be used by other computers to construct the device itself.

Soon Oki would be in favor once again. His status within the corporation would be insured. And his many enemies would be punished.

three

Gavin saw the red flannel flying from Kendall's window and knew that the mail was in. Gavin's hillside cabin was not subject to mail delivery, so all of his correspondence was delivered to Kendall's Book Store on Main Street. Kendall flew the red cloth from her bedroom window, which faced Gavin's hillside, whenever there was something for him.

It had not been going well with Kendall. He had finally told her the truth: how he had been a member of the CIA's Terminator Squad, how he had killed men that the CIA had pointed him at.

He had told her that his name was not Evans, as she had thought, but Gavin. He had told her that he was through with all of that. He had told her that he was ready to settle down.

She had told him to get out of her house.

Gavin didn't regret telling Kendall the truth. She deserved to know, especially if their relationship were to go any further. It had taken her a good two months after his confession to loosen up a bit. A month after that, she was almost social to him when he stopped by the Book Store.

In the last week, she had been downright friendly again.

So she had finally assimilated the bitter truth and was ready to move forward. Gavin was glad of that, but he had something else on his mind at the moment.

Money.

His stash was down, he had no income, and there was no work for him in High Card, Colorado, unless he wanted to tend bar at one of the lodges during ski season. All he knew how to do was kill, and no one was hiring.

That was one of the reasons for the car. He needed transportation, and with Dorn's help, he was going to get it. Gavin had checked the Trans Am the night before. The new engine had been installed and Dorn was planning to mount the wheels and tires that morning.

Gavin had a car that could do a hundred and fifty miles an hour, but he had nowhere to go.

It didn't do any good to dwell on it. Gavin got down on the floor and pumped out fifty sit-ups. He stood up, stretched out for a few moments, then did fifty pushups.

Next week, he thought, he'd start to run.

When he arrived at Kendall's she seemed concerned. He saw why when she handed him the mail. Atop the usual stuff was a cable.

"They brought it this morning," she said stiffly. She knew what cables meant. In the old days Gavin had been contacted through an ad run in the employment section of the *Wall Street Journal*. Now he was a civilian. He got his bad news in a cable, just like everyone else.

Gavin tore open the envelope and quickly read Coletti's message. "Damn," he said softly.

"What is it?"

"A friend," he said. "His name's Jack Duffy. He was pistol-whipped in San Francisco. Left for dead." Gavin shrugged. "He might be dead by now." He tapped the cable. "He was in a coma when this was sent out last night."

Kendall was going to say something about the senseless violence that permeated American society, about the homicide rates in American cities that eclipsed the murder rates in Third World hellholes.

But Gavin was already walking out of the

Book Store. "Where are you going?" She called out to him.

But he was already gone.

Dorn wiped his hands on the orange rag he carried in his back pocket as he led Gavin into the small room that served as his office.

"Another trip, huh?" Dorn pulled a bottle of Bushmill's from the lower drawer of his battered desk. He rinsed out two glasses in the bathroom sink, then poured double shots for each of them.

Gavin sipped the Irish whiskey, then put down the glass. He reached inside his jacket and withdrew a white envelope. Gavin handed the envelope to Dorn. It contained most of Gavin's cash.

"Getting kind of thin," Dorn said, as he hefted the slender package. Then he walked to his office safe, worked the dial, then opened it. He put the envelope in, slammed the door, and spun the dial. "You sure you're taking enough with you? Helluva thing to run out of cash on a trip."

"I'm OK," Gavin said, finishing his whiskey. "Let's get going. My flight's scheduled for three-thirty."

Later as Dorn's Bronco passed the season's first snowdrifts in the mountain pass leading to Denver, Gavin wondered if Duffy was still alive in that San Francisco hospital room. He would know soon enough.

Jimmy Shigata decided that two men should be enough, and had therefore selected Tsumoru Sasaki and Mitsuo Ishido to finish off Jack Duffy. Shigata explained that much depended on their mission, and from the expression on their faces, Shigata knew that they both knew exactly what depended on their mission: Shigata's ass.

But there was no question of them failing to carry out their orders, no matter how much they despised Shigata personally. They had been placed under his command, and they would not waiver.

Sasaki and Ishido, clad in sharkskin gray suits that fit snugly across the back and in the sleeves, left the warehouse at seven o'clock. When they returned, Shigata's latest problem would be solved. Duffy would be dead.

There was still the question of moving the girl. A blonde in the company of four Orientals was a bit too noticeable. They would have to wait for the heat to abate.

The two *yakuza* who remained—Kenzo Akutsu and Koichi Tomori—were sitting at the small wood table. Kenzo was dealing the cards. Shigata knew that they would play for perhaps an hour, the game ending in shouts and accusations of cheating. Then one of them would go out, buy some oriental delicacies, and return to eat with his companion.

Shigata had no stomach for anything but fried foods, tomato sauce, or cold meat sandwiches. He told the two thugs he'd return in an hour, and set out from the warehouse in search of a good Italian restaurant.

Gavin decided to go directly to the hospital from the airport. He would find a hotel later on. He wanted to check on Duffy, and that would be easier to do if he arrived during visiting hours.

Gavin took a cab into town, an unusual expense for him but justified by the circumstances. He had brought three thousand dollars in cash. Gavin couldn't keep his mind from calculating and adjusting his cash reserves. Money had never been a problem before, and it wasn't a problem yet. But Gavin could see it coming.

San Francisco Memorial Hospital was located near the Embarcadero. When the cab pulled up at the hospital entrance Gavin noticed the two blocky Japanese entering the building. When one of them reached out to push open the heavy glass door, Gavin saw that the man's pinky finger was missing.

Yakuza.

Gavin paid the cabbie and hurried into the hospital. His luggage consisted of one rather worn backpack made of blue nylon. He slipped the pack over one shoulder as he approached the information desk. He could see into the elevator well from the information desk; the two *yakuza* were waiting impassively for an "up" car.

"J. Duffy? That's three-twelve, but I'm afraid there's no visitors at this time. Perhaps you'd care to speak to the doctor in charge? You are family, isn't that right?"

Gavin gave the clerk a tight smile and hoped it was answer enough. He ran for the elevator, slipping in alongside the two *yakuza* just as the doors started to close.

On the floor selection board, number 3 was lit up in orange light. Gavin smiled at them, and they stared right through him.

Gavin turned and faced the elevator's double doors, his pack held carelessly in his left hand. Coincidences always bothered Gavin, especially where violence was concerned. Duffy was on the third floor, a victim of a brutal beating. Gavin was in an elevator, riding to the third floor with two men easily capable of administering that kind of assault.

Who were they there to visit?

When Gavin stepped out of the elevator the sign on the wall said that rooms 300–325 were to the right. He headed down the well-lit corridor, the footsteps of the two *yakuza* sounding behind him.

He stopped at the nurse's station and placed his pack on the counter. Seated behind the counter was a gray-haired woman in hospital white. "I'd like to see the doctor in charge of Mr. Duffy, the patient in three-twelve," Gavin said. Out of the corner of his eye he saw the *yakuza* pause in front of 312, then check out the corridor in both directions.

One remained posted outside the door while the other man entered the room.

Just as the head nurse started to answer him, Gavin turned and raced down the corridor. The *yakuza* outside the door to 312 saw him coming, his eyes widening in anticipation. Gavin heard the low savage growl in the man's throat as the *yakuza* squared off to meet his charge.

There was no time for a prolonged fight with the sentry. Gavin had to get inside as quickly as possible. The *yakuza* was poised to counterpunch, his weight evenly balanced on his feet, confident that the charging gray-eyed man would be an easy opponent.

Gavin started an overhead blow with the pack clenched in his left hand. When the smiling *yakuza* raised an arm to ward off that silly blow he was surprised with a quick kick between the legs, a ball-breaking jolt delivered with the tip of Gavin's reinforced boot that left the Oriental sitting on the floor, cupping his tender crotch with both hands. Gavin was through the door in the next instant.

The other *yakuza* was holding a pillow over Duffy's face when Gavin burst into the room. He turned to face Gavin, but he was off balance and the force of Gavin's charge took them across the room and against the window that overlooked the parking lot.

Gavin staggered the *yakuza* with a straight blow delivered with the heel of the hand against the *yakuza*'s nose. Blood erupted in a messy smear as the *yakuza*'s eyes rolled with pain. Gavin spun him, gripped the smaller man's hair and suit jacket, and threw him headfirst out the window, the *yakuza*'s scream filling the room.

Gavin heard the breathing behind him, but before he could turn there was a sudden cessation of sound, then a flash of red. Gavin crumpled to the floor.

four

"Feeling better?"

Gavin opened his eyes. The back of his head felt as if an anvil had been welded to it. He tried to sit up, but that action produced an intestinal 180. He laid back down, managing not to moan.

"I said, are you feeling better?"

Gavin was aware of a rancid tobacco smell along with the equally unappetizing odor of a wet wool overcoat. Gavin opened his eyes again and focused on a gray-haired man with an old-fashioned fedora pushed back off his forehead. One eye was squinting, avoiding the trail of smoke from the filter-tipped cigarette wedged into the corner of his mouth. Only the word *COP* tattooed across his forehead would have made him any easier to make.

"He did it with his hand," the gray-haired man said, smiling. "Pretty effective."

Gavin swallowed, relieved to discover that he was still capable of some action. "Who're you?" he said. His voice sounded far away, sleepy.

"Cooke," the man said, removing the cigarette from his mouth and depositing it under his shoe. "I'm a cop. I'm in charge of the Duffy investigation. So when you came in asking for Duffy's doctor and then ran off to cause mayhem, they called me."

"They were trying to kill him."

Cooke nodded. "The pillow was still on Duffy's face when the nurse got here. The guy who nailed you mangled a couple of orderlies on his way out. One of them's in intensive care."

Gavin said nothing.

"The other guy—the one that went out the window—he's oatmeal."

Gavin held his hand in front of his face and saw eight fingers.

Cooke stuck another cigarette in his mouth and flared a match. "Which brings us back to you," Cooke said, his narrowed eyes on Gavin. "You can talk to me now or you can talk to me later, but not much later."

"Let's do it now," Gavin said. The pain in his head was beginning to fade.

Gavin turned his head and saw Duffy in the bed next to him. Duffy appeared to be asleep. Except for the white bandages swathing his head, he seemed to be all right. But his breathing was almost impossible to detect.

"Who are you?"

"A friend of Duffy's," Gavin said.

"I'm touched, but I'd prefer a name."

"Evans," Gavin said. "Bob Evans."

Cooke was scribbling in his notebook. "Where you from, Bob? Out of town, right?" He pointed with his ball-point pen at Gavin's backpack, resting on the room's only chair.

"High Card, Colorado."

"What do you do there?"

"Auto restoration," Gavin lied. "Classic Cars Limited. Dorn Morrissey is the owner's name."

Cooke nodded. "So why are you in San Francisco?"

"I came to see Duffy." Gavin's head was beginning to hurt again.

"How'd you find out he was hurt? The only people that know about him right now are cops. How did you find out?"

"A cop told me."

Cooke put down his pen. "Is that right?"

"That's right," Gavin said. He closed his eyes against a sudden flare of pain. "And that's all I have to say. We both know I'm not a lead in this case. Let's cut the bullshit. My head hurts."

Cooke shut his notebook and eased his weight over to his left foot. "What do you know about Duffy? What kind of a guy is he?"

Gavin said, "He's clean. He walked in, saw something, so two goons were sent up here to clean him up. That's what I think."

Cooke nodded. "We don't know what to make of it." He paused. He usually didn't talk to people he was questioning, especially about what he personally thought about the case. But Gavin was different. It was almost like talking to another cop.

Almost.

"We don't have much connection between Duffy and the missing woman," Cooke said. "A couple of things—she's from the D.C. area, and so's Duffy. And she's missing, and he's half-dead."

"Those two guys that were here . . ."

"No I.D.," Cooke said. "Both Orientals, Japanese."

"Yakuza."

Cooke smiled. "Yeah. At least the guy on the pavement was. Unless he belonged to a strange cult that required the loss of a pinky."

"So he's a member of the Japanese Mafia. What's that got to do with Duffy?"

"We're working on it," Cooke said. He checked his watch. "The doc says you should be feeling better in about twelve hours. Maybe I'll stop back then."

"That would be wonderful," Gavin said, closing his eyes. He was asleep before Cooke was out of the room.

Mitsuo Ishido sat in front of Jimmy Shigata, his thick legs spread wide apart. Ishido had taken off his trousers and shorts, and was naked from the waist down.

His testicles were the size of oranges. His skin tone was green; almost twenty minutes of dry heaving hadn't made him feel much better.

Jimmy Shigata stamped out a cigarette and immediately lit another one. What the fuck else could go wrong? Sasaki is dead, Ishido's out of commission for quite a while, and Duffy's still alive.

Shigata glanced at Susan Billings. The adhesive over her mouth was still in place, but her legs had been freed from their bonds. She was now secured only by the wrists, each one tied to a corner of the bed frame. She lay on her back, propped up on a couple of pillows. Was she smiling at Ishido's discomfort?

"So tell me again, please," Shigata said.

Ishido groaned and recounted his tale. The sudden intrusion of an American and the commotion that he caused. How Ishido had barely been able to escape himself, what with the arrival of the orderlies as soon as Ishido had chopped down the American.

Shigata nodded. It was going to be all the more difficult to kill Duffy after this botched attempt. To make matters worse, other people were now involved—the orderlies that Ishido had attacked, the nurses. And there was Sasaki's corpse. It would be identified as that of a *yakuza,* due to their stupid practice of mutilating themselves.

If things were hot before, they were going to be on broil now. Shigata cursed, wondering if he was going to be held responsible.

And who was this jerk who fucked things up? What did he see that set him off? Was it just an unlucky break, or was there someone else involved now, someone who was just showing himself for the first time?

Shigata told Kenzo Akutsu, who was openly grinning at Ishido's expense, to help his stricken mate to the bathroom. There wasn't much to do until the phone call came.

When Gavin awoke, dawn was breaking and the room seemed chilled. He glanced at Duffy, who had not moved an inch. Gavin got out of bed slowly, rising first to a sitting position, then finally standing, on wobbly legs.

He washed up, then dressed. He drank a glass of water from the pitcher on the nightstand, took a last look at Duffy, and left the room.

The nurse at the station near the elevators had stood up when she saw Gavin walking down the corridor. "Inspector Cooke said—"

Gavin said, "Thanks. Tell Cooke I'll be in touch." There was an elevator car waiting on the third floor. Gavin was in it before the nurse got through dialing the police department's number.

Outside the hospital Gavin dug his down vest out of the pack and slipped it on. Early morning in San Francisco—gray and misty—was a damp, chilling time, but Gavin knew he'd warm up as he walked.

He finally took a city bus to Market Street and ate breakfast in a large cafeteria filled with construction gangs and other early-morning workers. He had scrambled eggs, sausage, English muffins, and a pot of coffee. He read the copy of the *San Francisco Chronicle* that he'd picked up at the corner newsstand.

There was no mention of Duffy. Justice Department muscle must have been applied to keep that story out of the paper. Gavin frowned. That was odd. First of all, it would take a lot of arm twisting on the part of the Justice Department to do that, and what would be the point? After all, Duffy didn't do anything wrong. He was the victim of an assault.

So why the news blackout?

At seven forty-five Gavin left the cafeteria, feeling a lot better. He still had a weakness in his legs, but the more he walked, the stronger they felt.

He hiked toward the Oakland Bridge, hoping that the Agency setup was still the same. CIA domestic operations, while technically against the law, were as common as jaywalking, which is also against the law. The Agency's resident in San Francisco ran a printing firm that specialized in full-color hardcore pornography.

The print shop was located ten blocks from the bridge, in an industrial section of the city seldom seen by tourists. Newspapers blew in the street—the look of hard-times unemployment was everywhere. Too many able-bodied men on the streets, wandering. Cafes, windows boarded over, out of business. Very little traffic.

Gavin pushed open the reinforced glass door and stood in a deserted reception area. It was a small room and contained a sofa against one wall and a coffee table covered with printing industry trade publications. There was no one seated at the receptionist's desk, on which had recently been installed a push button and a sign that said RING HERE.

Gavin pushed the button and thirty seconds later Charlie Mitchell came through the door from the workshop. He was a thin black-haired man with a large nose and close-set eyes. There was a nervousness in his manner that made him appear timid.

That was not the case.

Charlie Mitchell leaned on the doorframe and grinned at Gavin. "What the hell are you doing here? I heard that you sat down. Got fed up with the whole nine yards."

"I need some help," Gavin said.

Charlie turned and cocked his head, telling Gavin to follow him. Inside the workshop the roaring of the printing press made conversation impossible.

Charlie Mitchell's operation was totally self-contained. Photographers brought in the color transparencies, and Charlie's layout artists did the rest on a long table twenty yards from the press. Paste-up and stripping—preparing the magazine flats for the photographic process—were done by the same people.

A lone writer sat at a typing desk, grinding out blurbs and photo captions for the magazines.

Gavin followed Charlie Mitchell into his soundproof office. Charlie closed the door behind them, then sat down behind his desk. A stack of Charlie's latest magazine—*Pistons of Pleasure*—was on the desk.

Gavin sat in the chair facing him.

"So what is it?" Charlie Mitchell asked. His eyes were twinkling with information. He knew something and Gavin wanted to know what it was.

"I need a piece," Gavin said.

"That's it?"

Gavin shrugged. "A friend of mine's in trouble. Some *yakuza* are involved. That's about all I know. Except for the girl. Her name's Susan Billings, and she's missing."

Charlie Mitchell laughed. "Gavin, the piece will be no problem. I can get it here in a couple of hours. But let me give you some advice, free of charge. This is a big one. The NSA is all over it."

"National Security Agency? What the hell do they want with this?" The National Security Agency could be very nasty. Larger and more efficient than CIA, its operatives were generally even more elitist than either the FBI or CIA. NSA had almost unlimited power and resources, and the ruthlessness that went with a supersecret government agency out of control.

Charlie Mitchell enjoyed Gavin's surprise. "It's the Billings woman," Mitchell said. "They don't give shit one about Duffy. But Billings was involved in some sensitive work for an electronics firm in San Jose. Government stuff. The Defense Department's got its arm over the whole electronics industry. If you're working for some high-tech company, NSA is all over you. Plus, NSA's security man has disappeared. They figure he's dogmeat by now."

"That doesn't explain the *yakuza.*"

"No it doesn't. I have no idea what those characters are doing in the middle of this, and I don't want to know." He paused. "You like Walthers, don't you?"

"Sure. Any spare P-thirty-eights would be appreciated."

Mitchell stood up. "Stop by in a couple of hours. And don't say I never did anything for you."

Walking back towards the Tenderloin, Gavin thought about what he had learned. It was NSA, not the Justice Department, that had kept the story out of the newspaper. They could do it easily, and wouldn't hesitate either. Freedom of the press and other legalities were just so much irrelevant nonsense to those guys.

Gavin would feel a lot better once that automatic was tucked into his pack.

five

"Inspector Cooke?"

"Who's this?"

"Evans," Gavin said. He was using a pay phone on Geary Boulevard. Two men dressed like lumberjacks walked by, holding hands.

"You weren't supposed to leave the hospital. You know damned well I wasn't through with you."

"The place was depressing. Besides, I don't have anything for you. You have anything for me?"

Cooke was fuming. "Look, Evans. Things have changed since we talked. You've got to come in—now!"

Gavin hung up the receiver and stepped from the booth. NSA must have rung Cooke's chimes. The pressure Cooke was under was evident in his tone of voice. Dreams of pensions out the window. Gavin knew the reaction well enough. It was a common symptom suffered by government workers facing the prospect of early, involuntary, retirement. Nothing makes a bureaucrat more bushy-tailed than official pressure.

NSA wanted Gavin out of the picture, afraid that he would leave muddy footprints all over their clean little deal, whatever it was.

But NSA wasn't there because of Duffy; their concern was national security, whatever that was. They were worried about Susan Billings, not Jack Duffy.

Susan Billings hadn't saved Gavin's life, but Jack Duffy had. Gavin owed him whatever it took to square the deal. Duffy was down with his head cracked open; even sticking needles into Duffy wouldn't wake him up.

The people who did it would find that their payment would be painful and hard, administered by a cold-eyed man named Gavin who liked things to balance out.

At Brooks Brothers near Union Square, Gavin bought a dark blue wool blazer, two blue oxford shirts, and a maroon striped tie. A pair of dark gray wool slacks completed the outfit, along with a pair of black brogans, heavy-duty dress shoes suitable for both the boardroom and the alley. He changed into his new outfit in the store and packed his down vest, wool shirt, boots, and jeans in his pack. San Francisco was perhaps the most conservative city in America in terms of fashion. In a tie and jacket, Gavin would blend in.

His next stop was a luggage shop. There he purchased a sturdy American Tourister capable of holding everything in his pack, as well as the pack itself. He packed the dark brown valise, and walked three blocks to the Sir Francis Drake Hotel, south on Grant Avenue from Union Square. The hotel catered to the expense-account crowd, so by three-thirty the bar was crowded with men in gray suits and women laughing a bit too loudly.

Gavin booked a room and went directly to it. The name Evans was already useless—half of SFPD would be circulating through the city's hotels, looking for a cowboy named Evans who checked in with a backpack.

Gavin sat on the bed and hauled out the Walther. Mitchell had been as good as his word—even better. He'd provided fifty rounds along with the automatic, and a double-strap under-the-arm holster, a type Gavin had never before used. He eased his arms through the support straps, tucked the P-38 into the holster, and put on his jacket. He stood in front of the closet door mirror.

With the button fastened, there was an ominous bulge under Gavin's left arm. But with his jacket button unfastened, you couldn't see a thing.

As long as his jacket didn't flap open in a breeze.

It was definitely better than nothing, and as far as this deal was concerned, that was a step in the right direction.

Inspector Cooke ate two Gelusil tablets, then washed down the crumbs with a paper cup of water. He wiped his mouth as he tossed the cup into the receptacle beside the water cooler. Inside his office, the two NSA agents were talking. Cooke watched them gesture. One of them pounded the desk. Better get back in there, Cooke thought. He walked down the corridor made by the desks of the men working burglary. Most of them were in shirt sleeves, on the telephones. Others were reading newspapers or typing reports.

"Cooke," Agent Simpson said, "we don't hold you responsible for losing Evans. But you blew that phone call. You put a burr up his ass."

Simpson was a tall rangy man with dark blond hair cut short. His face was unremarkable except for a jawline scar. Curry, his partner, was a muscular, balding man with a five o'clock shadow that wouldn't go away no matter how often he shaved. Curry was pissed off, and Cooke knew it.

"We got one good lead in this fucking deal and you short out over the telephone," Curry said. He was blinking rapidly, trying to sort out his thoughts. "This guy Evans is a professional of some kind. Look how he vanished. Look how he took care of those two Japs in the hospital."

"We checked him out," Cooke said. "He is from Colorado. He does work for a guy named Morrissey who runs an auto restoration shop."

Curry snorted. "Listen, Cooke. Spooks are my business, not yours. This guy stinks to high heaven. What do I give a shit if he checks out? You don't realize how meaningless that is in our business. I'll make you a bet. You press down on that Evans I.D. of his and you'll find out how quickly it comes to an end."

Cooke didn't have to. He already had, as matter of fact, and Curry was correct. Bob Evans seemed to have hatched from an egg in High Card, Colorado. There was nothing that came before High Card. All the references that were on file in the small Colorado town came to nothing. Bob Evans was a sleeper, just now awakening.

"Look, what's done is done," Simpson said. "But we'd like some cooperation on this. Keep your men on the street, keep them looking.

He's probably still around. He wants in on this, so maybe he'll make a mistake."

Curry snorted again. "This guy is going to be hard. Don't think anything else about it. I smell spook all over this guy. I wish I had more on him. I'm positive we could make him in Washington—he's got to be in somebody's files."

Cooke nodded. Evans was a pro, all right. And that just made it even more difficult than it already was. Why did Duffy have to get nailed in San Francisco?

And why did he have to know Susan Billings?

Curry stood up and walked toward the door. "Washington's not happy with any of this," he said ominously.

Suddenly Cooke had had enough. "Washington's not happy? So what am I supposed to do? Eat my .38? This is San Francisco, not Washington. We got a missing person, and we got an assault case that could turn into a homicide. The rest of it is your trouble, not mine."

Curry rocked back and forth on his heels, then grinned. "If you really believe that, you're a bigger asshole than I thought you were."

Gavin had two beers in the hotel bar, then got a pocketful of change and called Dorn

Morrissey in High Card. Dorn answered on the first ring.

"How's it going?"

"What the hell are you up to? The place was swarming with cops this afternoon. Asked me if you worked here, and what did I know about you, and meanwhile they had their noses into everything in the shop!"

"How's the car?"

"Fuck the car! What the hell is going on?"

"A little trouble out here. I could really use that car. Is it running?"

"Hell yes it's running. Like a dream. I even installed that special console between the seats. And the landing lights."

"Any chance of you getting it out here?"

"To San Francisco? You want me to drive it to San Francisco?" There was disbelief in Dorn's voice.

"You're the mechanic. Don't you have any faith in your work? Besides, how long can it take? That thing's pretty fast, isn't it?"

"Yeah. Real fast."

"Put your money where your mouth is."

"Damn."

"And one more thing."

"One more thing? You want me to drive that damned car all the way to San Francisco, you had cops all over my case all day long, and there's one *more* thing?"

"Yeah. You remember that Uzi you showed

me? The one you bought at the gun show in Denver?"

"The Uzi."

"Bring it. We might need it."

It was a quiet evening on the third floor of San Francisco Memorial Hospital. Nurse Janet Springer was reading a romance paperback about a young woman who had inherited a rubber plantation in Peru. The novel's heroine was trying to sort out her personal life as she made agonizing decisions concerning the future of the business while being pursued by two incredibly handsome men.

Nurse Springer sat at the electronic console at the nurse's station. The quiet hum of the monitoring gear was lulling her to sleep. She yawned and glanced down the corridor, but there wasn't a soul in sight. Visiting hours had ended thirty minutes before.

The alarm for 312 sounded like an air raid siren in the quiet of the nurse's station. She picked up the telephone and got a message to Emergency, then replaced the receiver and set off on the double for 312.

The patient was in trouble. His heart fibrillation had the graph line on the heart monitor going all wrong. When the resident rushed into the room he took one look, then wheeled the electrical gear over.

The resident was good. It only took three

blasts of current to make Duffy stop dying. As soon as Duffy's heartbeat was steady the resident handed the electrical leads to Nurse Springer and for the first time noticed that she was a trim young blonde with a damned fine shape.

"Hi," he said.

"I don't date doctors," Nurse Springer said.

The two earlier beers had led to a total of four Scotch and waters. Then Gavin had gone down the street to a liquor store and bought a bottle of J & B to keep in the room. He was unsteady on his feet when he returned to the hotel. By the time he found his room and lay down on the bed, the room was picking up a nice spin.

He felt warm and secure, the alcoholic haze lulling him into a totally believable sense of well-being. He smiled at the ceiling and closed his eyes. There was no time to think about it. He was into it up to his neck. And while he still didn't know what the hell was going on, he knew that he would find out.

Gavin was back in business.

six

Jimmy Shigata hated to get up early in the morning. But there was no choice. Scanlon had specified that the meeting would take place at six o'clock; Shigata had arisen at five in order to shower and clear his head.

He was drinking his third cup of coffee in the breakfast cafe near Commercial Street when Scanlon came in, saw Shigata, and walked to his table.

The Chinese waitress brought Scanlon a cup of coffee as he sat down. He laid his raincoat on the empty seat to his left, then poured about three tablespoons of sugar into the coffee. He stirred, his frowning face averted from Shigata's gaze.

He put down the spoon, lifted his cup, and sipped coffee. The frown deepened, so he added more sugar and tried it again. Perfect.

When Scanlon finally regarded Shigata,

he plastered a big stupid grin across his face. "How you doin', Jimmy? Sure as shit is early in the morning. Ain't these mornings fan-fucking-tastic?" Scanlon pounded his chest with a closed fist. "You get off your ass early in the mornin', you get there while it's all quiet and nobody's around . . . damned fine time of the day!"

Shigata smiled and bobbed his head, an almost involuntary reaction to Scanlon's booming exuberance. Shigata wished he would shut up. Didn't he have any regard for being in a public place? Shigata couldn't understand people who acted as if they were the only person in a public place.

"Jimmy," Scanlon continued, lowering his voice, "things are going into the old shitter on this one. Now, boy, I don't have to tell you that there's a whole bunch of stuff ridin' on this deal. I don't have to remind you that your slice of the pie is pretty goddamned substantial. I sure as shit shouldn't have to ask if the girl's still alive, but the way things are going, I might as well."

"She's alive," Shigata said.

Scanlon nodded. "Well, she might not be for long. There's so much goddamned heat that she might have to go."

"No one said anything about killing her when I started this deal."

"Jimmy, Jimmy. No one's telling you to go

back there and kill her right now. Hell, she might live to see the turn of the century for all I know. Only thing is, you wouldn't want to see her on a witness stand pointing a finger in your face and saying, 'That's the asshole who kidnapped me.' That's what it could come down to, you know. Better clean her up if things get out of hand. For your own good, boy. For your own good."

"I don't mean I won't kill her. I mean, the deal didn't pay me enough to kill her. You guys want her dead, start talking numbers to me."

Scanlon grinned. "Jimmy boy, I'm goin' to let that slide. I ain't even goin' to report that you said it. Boy, you are about a cunt hair away from the big icebox. Don't go makin' threats. These boys will send someone down to that warehouse with enough hot shit for all of you."

Shigata was cursing the day he had gotten involved in the operation. It was supposed to be so slick—all that Japanese money behind them, a squad of tough *yakuza* to back him up. And all for what? Some stupid little piece of ass like all the others.

"So what am I supposed to do?" Jimmy Shigata said.

Scanlon said, "Just sit still. I'm here just to tell you that they ain't even near you. All that high-powered Washington heat is being spent chasin' that crazy that trashed your boys at the hospital. They got the police department doin' the same thing."

"Why is everyone so interested in that guy? Do they think he's mixed up in this?"

"Well hell yes!" Scanlon said, grinning. "Damned right they do! They want to bust *somebody*—anybody—because of all that heat. Hell, they had him in their hands and let him go."

Scanlon tossed some bills on the table, more than enough to cover their check. "So you stay tuned," Scanlon said to Shigata, his face suddenly cold and stern. "You might have to move pretty fast. You better be ready."

Gavin arose at nine o'clock, feeling well rested and refreshed. There was no trace of a hangover, and that made him smile. He showered and dressed, then left the hotel. The bulge of the Walther under his arm was less noticeable if he kept his jacket unbuttoned, and that was what he did.

He had a quick breakfast at a ham-and-egg diner on the corner of Market and Powell. Market Street, the city's widest thoroughfare, seemed less busy than he remembered it. Then he realized that BART—Bay Area Rapid Transit, or the San Francisco Subway—passed along Market Street. There were four subway stops along Market. The line connected San Francisco to the East Bay city of Oakland.

After breakfast he walked southwest on Market to the intersection of Haight. Gavin felt good, better than he had in months. There was the sudden surge of energy associated with danger, the feeling that the cobwebs were dropping away, cool freshness after a period of stale sameness. His senses were alive, alert. It was good.

He saw that Market Street had been changed. Wider than it used to be, due to the subway system humming along underneath the street. There were old-fashioned street-lamps along the street, and they were new as well.

At Haight Street Gavin walked two blocks west, then smiled when he saw the familiar hand-painted wood sign: HOGAN'S.

It was a basement bar, located down a flight of steps set flush with the sidewalk. The stairwell was framed by a six-foot iron spike fence, the spiked door leading to the stairs standing open.

Hogan's was a neighborhood tavern that threw the last customer out at two in the morning and let the drunks back in at seven, only five hours later. It was a hard-drinking joint, silent and chill, run by a man who hadn't touched a drop in over ten years.

"Beer," Gavin said, standing at the bar.

Hogan's eyes narrowed when Gavin entered, but he served the glass of lager and went on about his business. There was only one other patron, a short, stout man with a red nose and too much flesh around his waist. He put away three shooters of well bourbon, shook his head, and left.

Hogan walked down the bar to Gavin. "Long time since you've been around," Hogan said. "Everything OK?"

"Can't complain," Gavin said. Even though it was still early, the beer tasted damned good. He drained the glass and ordered another.

Hogan's eyes were wary. "You still with the outfit? I heard you pulled the pin a while back." Hogan's thick gray hair framed a square face.

"Hogan," Gavin said, "I'm up to my ass in a bad deal. I need some help."

Hogan got busy with his towel, stacking the glasses along the bar as he dried. "What the hell can I do for you? Hell, you know I'm not supposed to mess around unless it's company business."

"Hogan," Gavin said, "I need some I.D. real fast. I want it in any name at all except mine. It should be nice expensive stuff. Business cards and an AFTRA card. Make the business cards say that I work for CBS in

New York, and that I'm a line producer for 'Sixty Minutes.' "

"That ain't much," Hogan said. "That kind of shit won't hold up twenty seconds if they put you under a microscope."

"I just need it for one pass, in and out."

"Maybe I can handle it."

"Hogan," Gavin said, sucking down the last of his beer, "I'd appreciate it very much."

Inspector Dan Cooke stopped for a cup of coffee and a bear claw at a Winchell's Donut House located two blocks from Electrotec, Inc., near the outskirts of San Jose.

San Jose had changed quite a bit since 1957, the date of Cooke's last visit. The computer industry had made San Jose its capital. The San Jose/Santa Clara Valley area was better known now as Silicon Valley, a tribute to the computer industry's strength in the region.

The city had a curious look, a blend of the old and the new that seemed to be trying too hard. Cooke didn't like the New California look at all.

Cooke finished the bear claw, fired up a cigarette and sipped the coffee. The drive from San Francisco had given Cooke time to think. His mind worried over the case nervously, not able to let go. The National Security Agency was going to make trouble; Cooke didn't need trouble. NSA was hot about this one. Cooke knew why.

Cooke finished the coffee and deposited the paper cup in the receptacle near the glass door leading to the parking lot. Outside, the bright sunlight could not disguise the chill in the air. He felt old and stale. When he retired the first thing he would do would be to build a bonfire and feed it every suit he owned except the blue one he figured he'd be buried in.

By the time he had driven to Electrotec, parked in the visitors' quadrant, and presented himself to the smiling Eurasian receptionist, Cooke felt better. It was why he liked to work. It gave him a break from himself. Work immersed him in a reality out of control.

Inspector Cooke waited only five minutes before the solid wood door to the inner offices opened. The solidly built red-haired man standing in the doorway had a hostile face that gave way to an insincere but not ineffective smile as soon as he caught Cooke's eyes.

"Pleased to meet you," he said, extending his hand. His grip was dry and warm, almost as if he'd held his hands under a hot-air hand drier. "My name's Scanlon. I'm chief of security here. Mr. Edwards will be with you in a minute. Until then, is there anything I can tell you about the place?"

Cooke was unused to cooperation. It showed in his slow smile and wary manner. "Thanks, but I've just got a few questions for Mr. Edwards."

Scanlon's smile was still set on automatic, but his eyes were beginning to dart just a bit. "Maybe I could help you with that," Scanlon said. "What's it all about?"

"Susan Billings," Cooke said. "You're chief of security, so you know she's missing. Strange circumstances as well. We've got a man in a coma somehow connected to it."

Scanlon said, "Damnedest thing." He shook his head. The smile had been replaced by a Thoughtful Frown. "That's this business, though. That's why guys like me get good jobs in this business. Security."

Cooke nodded. "What's your main security concern?" he asked.

Scanlon said, "What you'd call trade secrets. All these outfits have research and development departments, and what those guys produce is what will make billions down the road a piece. Only there's a big market out there for their research. Other companies—other countries—will pay big bucks for new technology." His voice dropped to a whisper. "That's what happened to Susan Billings, if you ask me."

Cook hadn't, but he continued listening anyway. "That girl graduated from MIT with a doctorate in computer science and she is at the top in her field. Whoever snatched her will force her to cough up what she knows." Scanlon shrugged. "Probably the Japanese. They'll do anything to keep their technological edge."

"Is that right?" Cooke asked. Mr. Scanlon sure was a talker, now.

Scanlon checked his watch. "C'mon," he said. "Mr. Edwards should be ready."

Clayton Edwards was the chief executive officer of Electrotec and his office reflected his position. Fully carpeted in a brown earth wool rug, furnished with solid wood and leather chairs and a sofa. There was a bathroom to the right. Clayton Edwards stood behind a clean walnut desk, smiling at Cooke. "Come in," he said, waving Cooke to a chair. "Thank you, Scanlon," he said. The red-haired man nodded and left the room.

There was a computer console on display against the wall. Cooke didn't know if it was for show or whether Edwards actually used the damned thing. "I'm here about Susan Billings," Cooke said, opening his notepad.

"A shame. Have you found out anything?"

"We're working on it. What did Miss Billings do here?"

"She actually worked out of our San Francisco office and her home. She had a terminal in her apartment. She could work there if she desired."

Cooke nodded. "Pretty good deal. She's a young woman—how'd she rank such treatment?"

Edwards smiled. "Age has nothing to do with it. This is a young person's field. The president of Apple Computers is not even thirty years old. Miss Billings is brilliant in her field. She can have anything she wants when it comes to her work."

"What exactly is her work?"

Edwards sighed. "She is developing a rather sensitive device for us." He paused. "I'm only speaking openly because you have been cleared, of course."

"Of course," Cooke said. He knew that much of the work done in the Silicon Valley was top secret, Defense Department hardware and software and whatever the hell else they called it.

"Do you know what a VLSI is? A Very Large Scale Integration Circuit?"

Cooke shook his head.

Crawford frowned. "Look. Billings was working on a device called an Array Processing Encryption Device. In a nutshell, it's a coding device. It puts data into a form that is extremely difficult to decipher."

"Codes. Sounds like government stuff."

"It is. Whichever nation controls information, controls everything." He paused. "With the breakthrough that Billings achieved, things looked very good for us."

"Looked?"

Crawford nodded. "She could be forced to talk. Forced to duplicate her plans. Hell, she had diagrams in a microcassette. It wouldn't take long for whoever kidnapped her to check out her microcassette. That information would be worth a fortune on the high-tech market."

"Slow down a bit. Just what are the applications of this device that the Billings woman was working on? How valuable is it?"

Crawford smiled. "There is no outside dollar value. It's beyond that. The encryption device she was working on represents a dramatic increase in the capability of such devices." Edwards paused, aware that he had to explain things simply to Cooke, who didn't have a heavy technological background. "The device's uses are military communications, the transfer of funds for banks on the international level, and satellite data transmission in general."

"In other words, this encryption device is used damned near universally."

"Right. And the device that Billings was working on is years ahead of anything else. She's managed to take it all the way up to sixty-four K—it can encrypt data faster and more securely than anything we now have. And it's going to make the cracking of the other side's codes a piece of cake."

"It sounds like it's worth taking a risk for," Cooke said, "and it looks like whoever's got her is going to make millions of dollars."

Edwards said, "Exactly."

Gavin approached the intersection of Columbus and Bay. He had taken his time on the northerly walk, letting the sun-drenched day buoy him even further. The sudden clean vistas of San Francisco—white and blue and transparently beautiful—fed his new surge of energy. Gavin knew what was going on and he was surprised by it. This was the life that he had deserted, the life that he had thought drained him completely. Had he developed a psychological addiction to this bizarre life of danger? He didn't want to believe that. Danger junkies were a short-lived bunch who too often depended on balls instead of brains.

Gavin could see Susan Billings's apartment house from the corner. He lit a Marlboro, then eased into a phone booth that gave him a good view of the street. He held the receiver to his ear, nodding his head, checking out the pedestrians.

The street looked clean.

He replaced the receiver and tossed the cigarette into the gutter. He crossed the street at the corner with the rest of the law-abiding pedestrians, then turned down Bay. He walked past the apartment building on his first pass, came back down the other side of the street, then decided to get on with it. He ducked inside the building on his next pass.

Upstairs, Susan Billings's front door was easy to spot. The police tapes across the door had already been disturbed. That was often the case in apartment buildings. It took about two minutes to tumble the locks. Then he was inside.

The stain on the rug chilled him. It was Duffy's blood he was looking at, and it was a large, ugly stain. The sweet smell of blood was cloying his nostrils. He was trying to get a feel of the place, a sense of what had gone down.

From where Gavin stood he faced the kitchen, a small one-person affair. To his right was the living room, perhaps twelve by twelve. A short hall led from the living room to the bedroom, the door to which stood open.

Off the hall was the bathroom.

Gavin heard a noise. A low, indistinct sort of noise, perhaps a shower curtain settling into place, perhaps caused by the draft from an open window, perhaps nothing more than the crankings of Gavin's supercharged imagination.

Gavin crossed the living room silently. He reached under his left arm and pulled out the Walther P-38. Its weight felt comforting in his hand. When he reached the bathroom door he stopped, listening.

Nothing.

He entered the bathroom quickly, crossing the small room in two steps. His hand gripped the plastic flower-pattern shower curtain and he tore it open.

seven

She was beautiful. She stood in the bathtub, fully clothed.

Her eyes were round with fear, her red, full-lipped mouth open in breathless anticipation. Gavin realized he was pointing the P-38 between her full, upswept breasts.

"Hi," Gavin said.

"Don't shoot," she whispered.

Gavin slid the P-38 into its holster. "Wouldn't think of it," he said. "Not on the first date, anyway." He held out his hand and she gripped it with trembling fingers as he helped her step out of the tub.

There was a small dinette set in the kitchen—two wire chairs and a postage-stamp table. He sat her down, then took the other seat. "Who are you?" he asked. She was more beautiful when she wasn't frightened.

"Hillary Clarke," she said in a voice pitched a shade lower than Gavin expected. She had a growly sensual tone, the kind of voice he could listen to with pleasure.

"And?"

She must have thought he was a cop, because she kept talking. "I'm a friend of Susan's," she said. "I've even got a key to the place." She frowned. "I know I wasn't supposed to come in here, but I didn't see how it would hurt anything."

"It didn't."

"I just wanted to see if there was anything the police had missed. I mean, I *know* Susan! Maybe something would strike me, make me realize just what happened."

"Did it work?"

"No," she said. "I wasn't inside five minutes when I heard you at the door." She shot him a tentative grin. "So I hid in the bathroom."

"Tell me about Susan," Gavin said. He stood up and got an ashtray that was resting in the plastic drip-dry rack beside the sink. He offered Hillary a Marlboro and she took it. He lit it for her and watched her smoke. She wasn't very good at it, but she was trying.

"Well, you know. Susan's really smart and all that. I guess you know all about her work."

"Refresh me," Gavin said. "Tell me about it anyway."

"She was crazy about her job," Hillary said. "Even though the company was down in San Jose, they fixed up a bunch of equipment in her bedroom so she could work right here if she wanted." Hillary shook her head in amazement. "Imagine—a girl as beautiful as Susan, and a computer whiz too."

It did defy the imagination.

"What was she working on?"

Hillary's eyes rounded and glazed. Hillary was not a computer whiz, and Gavin could sympathize with that. "She used to show me," Hillary said, "but it never made much sense to me except the part about the codes."

"Codes?"

Hillary realized she had in front of her a person who knew even less about electronics than she did. She licked her lips as she began. "A lot of data is coded," she said. "That's what Susan worked on. Getting codes that would be impossible to crack. Whoever has the best codes controls information. Say the Russians break our code, but we can't break theirs. They'd have us!"

"Codes." Gavin's mind raced through his years in Washington. There was a name for it, if only he could remember. "Did she say what she was working on besides that? Was it a device of some kind?"

"Yes," Hillary said. She was sort of making a blueprint for it on her computer last time I saw her."

Then Gavin remembered. He sat forward suddenly and asked Hillary, "Did Susan say she was working on an encryption device?"

Hillary's big brown eyes opened wide. "That's it," she whispered. There was a note of marvel in her voice. "How did you know?"

"Top secret," Gavin said. "You had lunch yet?"

The Great Dane was puzzled at first, but when the thing started to move toward him he sensed the danger. There was no exit, and as Scanlon watched through the safety glass he saw the Great Dane circle the room, a few steps ahead of the robot.

There was no way out.

The Great Dane wasn't scared. He just didn't want to mess around if there was an easy way out. Satisfied now that he was going to have to attack this thing that was following him, the giant dog whirled, stiffened his front legs, and peeled his lips back from his fangs. He growled deep in his throat, then lunged forward.

It wasn't pretty. The robot gripped the charging dog easily in a cabled arm, then pinned the beast to the floor and began to dismember it, tearing the dog apart like a fried chicken in the hands of a hungry country boy.

Scanlon would call for the Maintenance Department to square away the room as soon as he got rid of the Great Dane's body.

"Very impressive," Clayton Edwards said. Edwards was a tall man, built like a long-distance runner. His short brown hair was precisely cut. He wore a gray suit of English wool, hand-tailored. Even white teeth were highlighted by a dark tan, the product of a visit to Tahiti. Edwards liked to get out of town every now and then. Executives needed to relax. Stress, he often said, was a killer.

Scanlon said, "We'll cut that robot loose at night. You won't have to worry about anyone poking around the offices."

The control device in Scanlon's hand was the size of a deck of cards. He flicked the controls to manual and backed the robot into the corner, then cut the power.

"Very impressive, I must say," Edwards said. "And now, if you please, a report on your meeting with Mr. Shigata."

Scanlon rubbed the heel of his hand over the beard growth on his chin. "Dumb little Jap's not worth the effort," he said. "If it was up to me we'd pay that little guy a visit and light him up. Him and those *yakuza* he's got with him."

"The Japanese are peculiar about violence,"

Edwards said. "Our contacts are already quite concerned over the extraordinary level of bloodshed already achieved. The electronics industry is a nest of thieves, but they prefer to keep their hands clean."

Scanlon shrugged. "It's all the same to me. I just work here."

"And now please tell me about the rest of the affair."

Scanlon walked from the safety-glass window to the desk. He sat down in a black leather chair and loosened his tie. "The Japs didn't want to go in because of the NSA surveillance. I had to get rid of the surveillance or nothing would have happened. So I did. How the hell was I supposed to know that that guy from the Justice Department—Duffy—was going to walk in right in the middle of it?"

"Do you mean to tell me that you were responsible for that NSA agent's disappearance?" There was a note of sudden stark incredulousness in Edwards's voice.

Scanlon's gaze was pure arrogance. "Cut the shit," he said. "We needed to grab that broad, damn it to hell. How in the world did you think it was going to be done? That boy had to go, and that's all there is to it."

Edwards was fussing with a pen. "But the NSA—"

"Look," Scanlon said, leaning forward, "that

boy is beyond identification. For all they know he was in on the kidnapping. All they know is that he's gone. Now somewhere up the coast they got a mutilated body in a morgue and maybe someone'll go up there and take a look at it, and maybe they won't. There ain't a helluva lot to see."

Edwards seemed to regain control of himself. Scanlon despised him. He was a big baby, afraid of a little blood. All he wanted was the money and clean hands. Scanlon wanted to laugh in his face.

"What bothers me," Edwards said, "is that it could all be for nothing. Perhaps we will have to eliminate the girl. In that case, kidnapping her in the first place was a completely useless act."

"Ain't that the shits," Scanlon said.

Gavin escorted Hillary Clarke home after lunch. She had a small apartment on California Street near the Golden Gate Park. She gave him her phone number and invited him in for a drink, but Gavin had work to do.

Thirty minutes later he was at Hogan's, and the gruff barkeep had Gavin's cards and AFTRA I.D. ready. He pocketed the manila envelope that contained his new identity, had a beer with Hogan, and left.

Gavin wondered how Duffy was doing. He knew that Duffy was in serious danger of never coming out of the coma. Even if he did come out, there was a chance that he would emerge from the subconscious darkness of the coma as a creature who bore little resemblance to the Duffy that Gavin knew.

The thought fueled the anger that Gavin needed to keep going. There wasn't much that got past his hardened exterior, but this did. Duffy was a friend, a man who had saved his life. He owed Duffy the whole ball of wax, and he would pay off.

Gavin returned to the hotel, checked the desk for any messages, knowing full well there wouldn't be any. But it paid to play out your role, he had learned.

Once inside his room he checked the cards that Hogan had given him. They were more than adequate. He placed the manila envelope on the nightstand, kicked off his shoes, and lay down.

Maybe Dorn would arrive in time to save him the expense of having to rent a car.

Susan Billings struggled against her bonds, but it was no use. Whoever had tied her to the bed was an expert. The cords were tight enough to make escape impossible, but not tight enough to restrict circulation. Her face flushed with effort, she relaxed, sinking back on the bed.

She tried working off the adhesive across

her mouth with her tongue, but all that produced was an aching jaw. It was hopeless. They had her and they could do anything they wanted with her.

What was particularly infuriating was the fact that Susan could hear street sounds filtering into the room. She knew that perhaps fifty feet away people were walking by the building, going about their business, living their lives. Whenever the door opened to admit one of the Orientals she was refreshed by a flash of light, sounds, and smells. Nothing would ever smell so exciting as the aroma of the street when the door was open—a smell composed mainly of rotting garbage.

Ishido, he of the swollen balls, came back into the room from the bathroom, still adjusting his fly. He glared at Susan, then smiled. He stood staring at her, his hands on his hips, his feet planted wide apart.

The front door opened and the little guy came in. He was American, Susan knew. She could tell that his Japanese was that of an American, faltering, badly accented. Probably second generation, she thought, trying to be more American than Jack Armstrong. The way he dressed told it all: running shoes, expensive jeans, cashmere pullovers, and plenty of gold chains. He looked like every San Franciscan's idea of a Southern Californian, i.e., an *Angeleno*.

It was a comforting thought, pinpointing him in her mind. It made him less fearsome somehow. He was whispering to the other man, and when they stopped talking and turned to face her, Susan's eyes grew round with fear.

She knew they were going to kill her. She knew it.

Kenzo Akutsu fumbled with the unfamiliar American coins, finally locating the one that fit the slot on the telephone in the lobby of the Sir Francis Drake Hotel.

He unfolded the slip of paper with the warehouse phone number. It had been an inspired moment when Shigata had assigned him to watch Susan Billings's apartment house on Bay Street. The man who had entered the apartment house that afternoon had obviously been wary of being observed. Of course, the man could not see Kenzo Akutsu, who was tucked up on a rooftop a block away scanning Bay Street with a high-power lens.

When the man had come out with the girl, Akutsu was already on the street, keeping them under visual contact. The man seemed taken with the young woman—hah!—and did not concentrate upon his task, which was to avoid surveillance.

Akutsu was able to follow them until the

man left the woman and hurried to a bar, then to his hotel.

Akutsu now had a name and a hotel room to go with the faceless menace that had interrupted Ishido and Sasaki at the hospital.

The phone was ringing, and Akutsu bit his lip as he waited for an answer. When Shigata's voice finally responded, Akutsu told him where he was, and what he had learned.

Shigata chuckled. "Very good," he said. "Remain there, unless he leaves, then follow him. We will join you as quickly as possible."

Akutsu replaced the receiver. He selected a bill from the roll that Shigata had given him and used the bill to purchase a newspaper in the hotel's tobacco shop. He pocketed the change, walked to the easy chair next to the sofa outside the bar, and waited.

eight

"I know driving up and down the hills is a pain in the ass," Gavin said. He was sitting on his bed, the phone tucked against his ear. "Meet me at Fisherman's Wharf. Anyone in town can tell you how to get there if you get lost. I'll be there in an hour or so. Just park the car and walk around. I'll find you."

Dorn had made excellent time—almost impossible time as far as Gavin was concerned. Dorn didn't know San Francisco at all, so Gavin didn't want the mechanic coming into the Union Square area. Dorn was phoning from a booth on Taylor Street. If Dorn drove north on Taylor he'd hit the waterfront and Fisherman's Wharf.

Gavin tossed his few items into the Tourister valise, shut and locked it. When he left the hotel, Gavin didn't notice the Oriental who fell in behind him. The hotel was near

Chinatown, and Akutsu was not the only Oriental on the street.

When Gavin got in a cab at the corner of Grant and Geary he still hadn't spotted Akutsu.

Fifteen minutes later when he stepped from the cab in front of Fisherman's Wharf, he missed Akutsu again, giving the Japanese time to place another phone call.

It took Jimmy Shigata fifteen minutes to get to Fisherman's Wharf. He saw Akutzu as soon as he turned down Jones Street. He quickly parked. He could see that Akutzu was still trailing their man, who Shigata could now pick out of the crowd. Shigata told the *yakuza* with him to be prepared for action.

Shigata fell in step with Akutzu, the third *yakuza* taking a position directly behind them. Just keep him in sight till he gets somewhere nice and quiet, Shigata thought.

But if it looked like they'd been spotted, Shigata knew he was going to have to take out the clown wherever he was.

Shigata didn't want to think about that.

Inspector Cooke finished his second pack of cigarettes at ten minutes past ten that evening. He crumpled the package and hookshot it toward the round file in the corner.

Detectives had been dragging in people all

day long, grilling them harshly, then moving them out to make room for the next load. Cooke had faith. Someone was going to know something about the *yakuza*. Someone was going to have seen them. He knew it.

Only he didn't enjoy the waiting. He tore open a fresh pack of Winstons, fed one into the corner of his mouth, and checked the wall clock again. Ten-fifteen.

Meehan walked in and sat down next to Cooke's desk in the straight-back office chair. His tie was loose around his neck, his breath stank from too much coffee and tobacco. "We got something," he said to Cooke. Meehan was a man Cooke's age who never let things get him excited.

Cooke walked down the corridor with Meehan at his side. "He's in number four," Meehan said. When Cooke arrived at interrogation room four, he stopped, dropped his cigarette, and ground it out before going inside.

His name was Dick Dempsey. Cooke nodded at him when he entered the room. Dempsey was a familiar face in Cooke's life, a small-time operator with fringe connections to one of Chinatown's more important tongs. The tongs, Chinese organizations that ran commerce—both legal and illegal—in the Chinese community, sometimes had need of a

Caucasian to clean up minor details. Dempsey was their man.

"Inspector," Dempsey said, a smile crooking his tight lips.

"Let's have it," Cooke said. He wiped a hand across his forehead and frowned with distaste as the accumulated grit and grease of a sixteen-hour day transferred to his palm.

"Like I was tellin' him," Dempsey said, pointing his chin at Meehan. "I heard about some Japs movin' in from one of my boys." Dempsey shrugged. "You know how it is. Japantown is one thing, but those three-fingered bozos is somethin' else."

Japantown, a relatively new commercial and financial center in San Francisco, had posed no threat whatsoever to the power of the tongs. The arrival of free-lance *yakuza*, however, was a different story.

"So?" Cooke asked.

"So if I was you," Dempsey said, "I'd be stickin' my nose in along Commercial street, nearby to Montgomery." He shrugged. " 'Course, I don't know if them's the boys or not. But they the ones I heard about."

Cooke smiled. It was going to feel real good to lay one on those clowns from NSA, with all their high-tech horseshit and bullying Federal Authority. He'd nail the *yakuza* and make those two jackasses come to him for answers.

* * *

Scanlon parked almost in front of the storefront on Commercial street. He sat in the car, scanning the street. It was quiet—not a pedestrian in sight. He screwed on the silencer, then got out of the car.

He hoped they were all there. He liked to pop people in a row, like squeezing plastic blisters in packing material. One kill just didn't do it.

Scanlon walked to the door and knocked. There was no sound from inside; for a moment he thought that they had packed up and marched.

But then the peep slid open and a pair of oriental eyes regarded him carefully. Scanlon grinned, and the door opened.

There was only one *yakuza* inside. He said something to Scanlon in Japanese, but Scanlon didn't speak Japanese, so he just kept smiling, nodding, while he scanned the room. The Jap was alone, and the bound girl was regarding him with recognition in her eyes.

Satisfied that they were alone, Scanlon set his attaché case down on the table, flicked the lock controls, and lifted the lid. The Jap was all eyes when Scanlon pulled the silenced automatic from inside. He was still staring at the weapon when Scanlon squeezed off a round that caught the *yakuza* in the throat and spun him around. His blood trailed a red arc on the storeroom floor. Scanlon pumped another round into the Japanese's back. When the *yakuza* flattened out on his face Scanlon stood over him and turned the *yakuza*'s head into gumbo.

Scanlon could hear the soft moans of Susan Billings as she witnessed the execution. He turned to her and smiled. She managed to keep her gaze on his face as he walked toward her. When he put the silencer's tip—still hot—about an inch from her forehead her eyes began fluttering.

He peeled off the adhesive and said, "One sound and you and that boy over there will be traveling the same path, little lady."

She nodded dumbly, her mind trashed. "Now we're just goin' to get up and walk right outta here," Scanlon said. "I got a nice car parked outside and when I open the trunk I want you to step right inside like a good girl. You got that?"

Susan nodded again. Her tongue was dead in her mouth, a frozen muscle. She couldn't swallow and could barely breathe. The miasma of evil surrounding Scanlon was thick as sheep's wool.

Scanlon untied her hands, then let her get slowly to her feet. She was shaky, her muscles in spasm from the restraints. Scanlon didn't want to know about it. "Just move it," he said, gesturing with the gun. "I'd just as soon turn you over right here," he added, and Susan Billings believed him.

Outside, the street was deserted. Scanlon opened the trunk and Susan Billings got in. He slammed shut the lid, then got behind the wheel.

The damned deal was getting crazy and Scanlon didn't know what to do about it.

The fog was thick at Fisherman's Wharf, but that only added to the waterfront's charm. The sidewalks were crowded with tourists and San Franciscans alike, some eating seafood cocktails sold on the street, others waiting for a table in one of the wharf's fashionable restaurants. There was the usual collection of young lovers, straight and gay, and a few roughneck fishermen giving the place an authentic touch.

Gavin decided to have dinner when Dorn arrived. He would treat the hulking mechanic to a blowout meal at Alioto's, then drive him to the airport for a return flight to Colorado. There was no point in Dorn staying on, and perhaps getting hurt.

Gavin walked slowly through the crowd, his senses suddenly aware of danger. He didn't waste time trying to figure out what had pricked his consciousness. He concentrated his attention on his immediate surroundings.

Gavin crossed the street and walked toward a three-masted sailing ship tied up at a pier. The ship was a tourist attraction, but what interested Gavin was the small, well-lit arcade opposite the ship. As he approached the arcade he saw that it was a video parlor, jammed with game-happy adults and teenagers feeding quarters into the machines. He glanced behind him and saw the three Orientals closing quickly.

He didn't care how they had picked him up. That was history. What mattered now was surviving the encounter.

Gavin knew that the *yakuza* liked to kill in the dark. Their operation so far had been as circumspect as possible. He figured they wouldn't make a move until they could get Gavin alone.

Gavin was wrong.

He entered the arcade, conscious of the heat and the musical electronic noise. There was a layer of smoke trapped against the ceiling and the air was compressed, claustrophobic. He edged through the crowd, the Walther tight under his left arm.

The three Orientals entered, trailing Gavin by perhaps fifty feet. They stood just inside the doorway, peering through the crowd. Jimmy Shigata saw Gavin first and nudged Akutzu, standing to his left. The third *ya-*

kuza's eyes followed the other eyes to where Gavin was standing.

Each of the three unpacked .45 automatics. The tall thin man behind the change counter yelled, "Hey!" Then some people in the crowd saw what was about to take place and their screaming stampede gave Gavin a moment in which to wedge himself behind two machines.

Gavin hauled out the Walther as a .45 slug tore past his head with the sound of an armor-plated bee. Gavin squeezed off two rounds and watched as one of the Orientals clenched his throat in a vain attempt to staunch the jets of thick, dark blood. One of the remaining Orientals broke for cover and the third one dropped straight to the floor, offering a difficult target.

Gavin put two rounds in his forehead when he looked up from the floor. The force of the slugs left the Oriental's head twisted at a bizarre angle. The dead man's feet twitched and the floor became wet with blood and urine as his involuntary muscles let go.

The arcade was filled with the sounds of screaming and the bittersweet aroma of gun smoke. So far no one had been hit except the men Gavin had shot, but the free-fire zone covered the doorway and no one could leave.

There was the wail of sirens coming closer.

The third Oriental broke for the door and Gavin sighed carefully, but there were too many people suddenly moving. At the last moment he lifted his sights and watched as the small, thin man dressed in designer jeans and running shoes darted from the arcade.

And then suddenly someone turned out Gavin's lights.

nine

They came down Commercial Street from both ends, sealing off the exits. A SWAT team led the way. Ten minutes later Inspector Cooke was standing inside the warehouse, checking out the dead body on the floor. He glanced at the bed in the corner. The restraints were still in evidence. Cooke knew this was where they'd been holding the girl.

But where the hell were they now?

The corpse had been walking and talking not too long ago—Cooke could tell that immediately. The guy was still warm. He sniffed the air. There was a trace of cordite.

"Bag him," Cooke said to the squad leader. Cooke was tired. Let someone else handle the meat wagon, the body bags, and the rest of it.

Cooke lit a cigarette. There was a commotion at the door, and then Curry and Simpson, the NSA agents, were inside the room.

"Well, well. And what do we have here?" Curry's eyes glistened in the harsh light. "Looks like you got here a hair too late," he said to Cooke. "Looks like maybe there's a security leak in your office. You no sooner decide to move in, and the bad guys move out." Curry prodded the corpse with his foot. "All except this guy. Who is he?"

Cooke shrugged. "Just another pretty face," he said. "This damned thing is out of control and you know it."

Curry and Simpson smiled. "Now look, Cooke," Simpson said, "there's a lot at stake here. Don't take it personally. We're in charge of security for Billings, but they took us by surprise. We've already lost one man. We've also lost what we were supposed to be securing."

"The girl might still be alive," Cooke said. "It looks like they were keeping her here. Moved her out a few minutes before we got here."

"Makes me feel warm all over," Curry said.

Cooke had had it. He opened his mouth to tell Curry to bite the big one when Meehan double-timed into the room.

"Gunfight down on Fisherman's Wharf," he said to Cooke. "Orientals involved."

Cooke, Curry, and Simpson exchanged looks. "Let's move," Cooke said.

Gavin awoke in Puke City.

Luckily the window on the passenger's side of the car was rolled down. Gavin rolled towards it, relieving himself neatly, finally gasping for breath. They were on the Golden Gate Bridge heading for Sausalito. Dorn was driving.

"What the hell happened?" He asked Dorn.

"By the time I got there you'd already been sapped by the owner, and the cops were about five blocks away. I ran in shouting Police!" and the owner pointed to you and said you were the only one left alive. I slung you over my shoulder and told the owner to keep everyone there till the other officers arrived. He was so shook up I guess he figured he'd better do like I said."

Gavin touched the back of his head. His fingers came away wet and sticky. "Bastard broke my head," he said. His head felt like it was caught in a vise. His stomach felt like he'd just eaten twenty chili dogs made from real dogs. The traffic ahead of them danced. He was having trouble focusing his eyes.

"How'd you spot me?" Gavin asked.

"Traffic was pretty bad when I got to the wharf, so I figured I'd drive around and see the sights. I saw you when you cut into that arcade. By the time I got there all hell had broken loose. There were people streaming out of the place, screaming and yelling. When I walked in I figured I'd best get you outta there as fast as possible."

"I didn't think they'd open fire in that arcade."

"Who's 'they'?"

"Japanese mafia. They're called *yakuza*. They've kidnapped the niece of a friend of mine. They put him in the hospital with severe head injuries. He's in a coma."

"They ain't playin' around."

"No."

"You coming back to Colorado with me?"

"I can't do that. I've got to see this thing through."

"Why? The cops and the FBI should be handling the kidnapping and there's not a damned thing you can do for your buddy in the hospital."

"It's not officially a kidnapping—no ransom note. The FBI isn't involved. And SFPD is in over its head."

A light rain started to fall and Dorn hit the wipers, which immediately smeared across the windshield. "Need new blades," Gavin said.

"You didn't answer me," Dorn said. "What the hell are you going to do here? Those guys are playing awfully rough. It's not like a barroom brawl, where you can handle yourself with your fists or a barstool. They'll blow you outta the water soon as look at you."

Gavin's head was pounding, his stomach doing flip-flops in time with the windshield wipers. "Just let me get a night's sleep," Gavin said. "We'll both feel better in the morning."

Inspector Cooke stood beneath the streetlight outside the video arcade, watching as the coroner's unit bagged the two bodies. The attendants worked quickly, moving the corpses with practiced ease. Feldman, from the coroner's office, stood by with a steaming cup of crab meat in his hand. "Been a long time since I've been down to the wharf," he said to Cooke. "I ought to come more often. Great stuff," Feldman said, chewing crab.

Cooke lit a cigarette, flipped the match into the gutter, and watched as a uniformed patrolman escorted the arcade owner to Cooke. "He laid out one of them," The patrolman said. "But some cop in plainclothes came in and hauled the guy away."

"That right?" Cooke asked.

"Yeah. I was in the back, working on the books. I hear all the shit coming down and by the time I get out I see one guy running out and this other guy watching him go. This one guy, he's still holding a gun, so I dumped him."

"And?"

"What do I know?" The owner shrugged. "Some guy runs in, says he's a cop. There's sirens all over the place, so I figure he's real. He lifts the other guy up and leaves. Tells me to secure the place till the rest of the cops arrive."

"Can you give us a description?"

"Sure. The one guy, the one with the gun, regular size, regular build, regular clothes. Brown hair, I think. Maybe thirty, thirty-five years old."

Cooke felt his head beginning to ache. "And the other one?"

The owner's eyes opened wide. "A fucking giant," he said. "Maybe six six, maybe two-fifty, two-sixty. A fucking football player. He was wearing jeans and a plaid wool shirt. Boots too. Brown hair and a brown beard." The owner concentrated, dreging his memory for details. "That's it," he said.

The dead men were *yakuza*, and the gunman that got away sounded a lot like Evans, but there was no way to be sure. Cooke had no idea who the giant was. Just another complication in an already upside-down deal.

The newspapers were going to have a field day with this bloodbath, smack in the middle of the hottest tourist area in town, when San Francisco is doing everything it can to bolster tourism.

Cooke tossed his cigarette into the gutter, got in his car, and drove back to the station.

It was going to be a long night.

ten

Two days to go.

Clayton Edwards sat behind his desk in the executive wing of Electrotec. He licked his dry lips, passing his tongue over the top, then the bottom. Excitement was a new sensation for him. He didn't know if he liked it or not.

The excitement of soon acquiring $750,000 was a pleasurable excitement, one that had distinct sexual overtones. With that kind of money, he could live as he pleased, where he pleased. Edwards knew what it would be like: a secluded palatial estate in a certain corrupt Third World locale. His money would buy official cooperation. Any excesses he committed could be covered up, easily forgotten. There were a lot of things Clayton Edwards wanted to do, and most of them were unpleasant. Children fascinated him, but only as sexual objects. He longed to give vent to every fetid, debauched wet dream in his mental garbage pail. The money would help him do it, because he would be living in a place where you bought people.

Yes. That was good excitement, a pleasurable longing soon to be realized. Clayton Edwards liked that.

But now there was the other thing—the excitement of fear. It filled him with horror. Clayton Edwards was a physical coward, easily intimidated by the use of force. Scanlon already knew that and was trying to bend Edwards to Scanlon's implacable will.

Ever since the Justice Department official, Duffy, had gotten involved in the situation, Clayton Edwards had been aware of an advancing feeling of dread.

The operation was off schedule. Unscheduled events frightened Clayton Edwards.

Billings was going to be so easy. With the help of the *yakuza*, whose efficiency had been extolled by Oki, Billings was to have been kidnapped, then transported to Japan. There she would be used as a blonde sexual treat. Men with enough money to meet the price could have a long-legged blonde, at least for the evening. According to Oki, films would of course be made; the *yakuza*, who ran such operations in Japan, would profit immensely from Billings's forced prostitution, as well as from the large fee they would be paid for kidnapping her.

Once Billings had been kidnapped, the encryption device data would be sold by Clayton Edwards to Oki, who worked for a consortium of Soviet-Israeli interests.

Clean. Simple. Billings is assumed to be the leak, when, shortly after her abduction, American intelligence picks up information indicating that the encryption device is out of the bag.

Clayton Edwards would be home free, and long gone.

But the immediate involvement of the San Francisco Police Department skewed the plan. Scanlon was righteously outraged. The operation was going to be worth $250,000 dollars to Scanlon—if everything finally worked out.

Edwards picked up a copy of *Japan Watch*, a newsletter concerned with technological development in Japan. He scanned the page thoughtfully. It dealt with Japanese advancements in supercomputers—the Fujitsu Vector Processor and the Hitachi M280H. Edwards frowned. The Japanese were locked in on technological superiority. They've already caught up with us. How long will it be before they pass us? Edwards smiled.

It's all going east anyway. I might as well get in on the ground floor.

* * *

Dorn pushed back from the table, covered his mouth as he belched, then poured their glasses full of wine. "Salud," he said, raising his glass. On the table were the remains of an All-American Steak Dinner—sirloins, fries, and salad. Dorn and Gavin were in the Beefhouse, a red-checkered-tablecloth road-house off Highway 1, north of Sausalito.

"Now let me see if I got this right. Your old friend Duffy gets fucked up, and his niece gets kidnapped."

Gavin sipped the red wine, his eyes tracking across the room. They were safe. The vibrations in the steak house were peaceful, pleasant. No hint of darkness.

"So you feel like you have to make this whole deal right somehow. Don't matter to you that some weird Japanese Mafia is involved. Hell no. That don't matter at all. It don't matter that your friend Duffy is on his own. There's not a damned thing you can do for him now. He either makes it, or not. And his niece—I guess you figure you can do a better job than the authorities on that."

Gavin leaned forward. "Dorn," he said. "That's got nothing to do with it."

Dorn's eyes widened. He finished the glass of wine, and then refilled their glasses. "Well then, what in hell does?"

Gavin was letting the wine take over. His

defenses were down and he knew it. Fuck it, he thought. You can't be on duty twenty-four hours a day. He had no idea when he'd be able to relax again, so he wasn't going to spoil this one. He drank from his glass, feeling warm, secure.

"Dorn," he said. "Duffy pulled me out of a real tight deal. Real tight. I owe the man my life. For some reason, he got himself jammed into the middle of a kidnapping. He had nothing to do with it. I think he was just in the wrong place at the wrong time. His niece—I don't even know her. I don't wish her any harm, but her well-being is not my concern." Gavin felt like a pompous ass. He didn't mean for it to come out like that. Must be the wine.

Dorn twirled his wineglass slowly. "This sounds like a real asshole deal to me. It don't matter if you single-handedly eliminate every goddamn *yakuza* from here to Honolulu. Duffy's either going to make it, or not. And you don't give a damn about the girl. So why all the excitement?"

It was hard to explain. Dorn didn't know much about Gavin—didn't even know his real name. But he knew that Gavin was a strange-enough man, given to suddenly leaving High Card and sometimes returning the worse for wear. He knew that Gavin had no steady employment, but had a few bucks nevertheless. Dorn didn't give a damn one way or the other what it was Gavin did for a living.

"Look," Gavin said. "I've got to do it. I'd prefer to be curled up at Kendall's with a whiskey and a stack of science fiction novels. I'd even prefer to be digging you out of a snowbank. But I've got to do it."

Dorn put his glass down. "OK. So where do we go from here?"

"I'll put you on a plane and head back to San Francisco. I've got to get down to San Jose and check that operation out. That's as far as I go."

"Good plan."

Gavin was annoyed. "It's no plan at all and I know it. But there's not much else to do. Besides," he said, pausing to finish the wine, "the other side doesn't have a plan either. I can smell it. They're winging it, just like me."

eleven

When Jimmy Shigata deplaned at Los Angeles International Airport—LAX—he half expected to be met by a few of the guys. There was no one present when he entered the arrival gate. He walked to the stairs leading to the lower level, then hiked down the endless corridor to baggage claim. It was a cool day, overcast, yet his armpits were dripping.

Jimmy Shigata was returning to Los Angeles a loser.

He probed an aching tooth with his tongue. In the last few days he had begun to hurt everywhere. His right arm was stiff with tension, his shoulder joint sore and aching.

I'm fucking falling apart. All because of that bastard who messed up the Duffy hit. We could've nailed him. We had him. Three to one. The fuck turns out to be Deadeye Dick.

Shigata claimed his luggage, then walked through the checkpoint that led to the taxi stands outside the terminal.

Once settled in the back of a Yellow Cab, Shigata reviewed his defense. He was going to have to be good, real convincing, or he'd be in big trouble.

He tossed his cigarette out the window. His mouth was dry as dust. What would they ask him? If he could figure out what they'd ask him, he'd have his answers ready. He wouldn't stumble around trying to think of something to say.

They'd ask, "What went wrong?"

Shigata closed his eyes, grimacing. What didn't go wrong? He had been cautious. Shigata had told Scanlon he wouldn't kidnap the girl until the apartment was no longer under surveillance.

Scanlon had been the one who had told Shigata the apartment was clear. Scanlon had told him that the surveillance agent was no longer a concern.

So I went in. It was perfect. We had her cold. Then this round-faced guy walked in. I wasted him. His skull was open, for chrissakes! I didn't put a bullet into him because there was no need to. We didn't want to attract attention, so I didn't shoot!

Shigata saw it then. He realized that there was no way around it. They would hold him responsible, because he didn't make sure. He didn't make sure that sucker was dead, and because he lived, everything else happened.

Jimmy Shigata stuck another 100-millimeter cigarette into his mouth. It was going to be no fun at all at the meeting. No fun at all.

Clayton Edwards was a nervous wreck.

"Just keep cool," Scanlon said. Edwards was pacing the floor in his office. Scanlon sat in the leather armchair by the desk.

"I'm trying to keep cool," Edwards said. His strained look denied his words. "We're so close—so close! Why the hell did you have to take the girl?"

Scanlon stared at Edwards. He had already gone over this once. How many times did Edwards have to hear it? "I got word from Meehan," Scanlon told him, "our man in the police department. He phoned and told me that they were on the edge of making some guy talk, and the guy knew where the Japs were holding her. That meant that they were going to take her that night. I had to get there before the cops did."

"And the man you killed?"

"I can't speak Japanese and he couldn't speak English. He didn't trust me—the only contact I had with that crowd was through Jimmy Shigata, who wasn't there." Scanlon shrugged. "The Jap came at me. I had to take care of him on the spot."

Edwards looked green. "There was to be no violence in this affair," he said, slumping into his chair behind the desk. "Now there are more people dead than I care to contemplate."

"And it's not over," Scanlon said. He couldn't resist. He loved the look of wide-eyed anxiety that it produced in Edwards.

"Where is she now?"

"She's at my place. She's tranked out—gave her the shot myself. She'll be asleep till three or four this afternoon. But I have to figure out what to do with her then. Can't keep her around all tied up and gagged. Besides, she knows who I am—she's seen me around here dozens of times."

Edwards nodded.

"Any suggestions?" Scanlon said. He could barely keep the look of mirth off his face.

Edwards looked exhausted. He waved a hand weakly. "Just don't tell me about it," he said to Scanlon. "Don't tell me about it."

Scanlon smiled. "Relax," he said to Edwards. "Everything's going to be A-OK."

On the drive to the airport south of San Francisco Gavin tested the '74 Trans Am. It was everything Dorn had said it would be. Fantastic acceleration, excellent handling. He wondered what Dorn had done to the suspension. Gavin had cranked the Trans Am to a hundred thirty miles an hour on a stretch of deserted road in Marin County, where they had spent the night, and it handled like a race car.

The console was a marvel. At a glance it appeared to be the standard console housing. With the push of a button the console lid lifted, revealing the Uzi.

He hadn't tried the landing lights yet. He would need another deserted road for that one.

"I still think I should stay," Dorn said.

"Well then, pick up the Uzi. When we get to the airport. I'll indicate a group of people to you. Use the Uzi on them."

"What?"

"That's what staying is going to be about. People you don't even know will be shooting at you, so you'll be shooting back. After a while, you decide it's safer to shoot first. It gets weird."

Gavin had to remember that Dorn had never been in the service. Dorn didn't have the faintest idea of what a firefight would be like. He would stand there with his mouth open, presenting the biggest target since King Kong.

"Besides," Gavin continued, "I need a base

camp in High Card. That's where I need you."

Dorn shook his head. "What an asshole world this is," he said.

Jimmy Shigata stared at the cauterized stump of his left pinky. His heart rate was thundering in his ears and he felt dizzy, nauseated.

Two Yakuza, their shirts off, their tattooed bodies lewd in the dim light, held Shigata's arms. It wasn't necessary. Shigata didn't have the strength to squeeze a pimple. He couldn't believe that they had done it to him.

At least it had been fast. They didn't waste time with a question-and-answer period. They grabbed him as soon as he walked in, pinned him in the chair, and chopped off his finger.

Shigata felt high, hashed out. Only he knew this was the real thing.

Mr. Oki was seated directly in front of Jimmy Shigata. Clad in a gray suit, highly polished black shoes, a white shirt, and a maroon tie, Mr. Oki's thin face seemed made out of stone. "You are fortunate," Mr. Oki said to Jimmy Shigata. "You will be given a second chance."

Jimmy Shigata swallowed, but said nothing.

"This time you have but one mission," Mr. Oki said. "That is, the elimination of those that stand in the way. The man known as Evans must not be allowed to cause further delay."

Evans. He was the bastard who had screwed up Duffy's assassination. The same bastard who had almost killed Jimmy Shigata in the video arcade.

What the hell did Evans have to do with any of this? Shigata's thought processes were fogged with shock and pain. It started out so simply. Kidnap a blonde girl; transport her to Mr. Oki for eventual sale in Japan. Shigata sold girls all the time. But he didn't kidnap them. He would lure them to Japan with contracts for show business jobs—dancers and singers. Once in Japan, the girls would discover what the truth was.

Shigata was thinking rapidly, trying not to let the reality of his situation sink in. He didn't want to freak in front of Mr. Oki.

He didn't understand Mr. Oki at all. Oki wasn't perturbed a bit by Scanlon's excuse for killing the *yakuza* guarding Susan Billings. Scanlon had said that the *yakuza* attacked him, and Scanlon had to move fast because the police were on their way to the warehouse on Commercial Street.

The cops were there all right. Scanlon must have a pipeline into the department. Scanlon beat the cops there by about fifteen minutes.

The throbbing in Shigata's stump made

him blink quickly to cut through the pain. All he had to do was take care of Evans. He would keep that front and center in his mind—just take care of Evans.

Then everything would be OK.

Inspector Dan Cooke rubbed his eyes, then checked the latest report on the video arcade firefight. The two addresses found in the dead Japanese's pockets had been checked out. One was for a neighborhood tavern called Hogan's, on Haight, and the other address was an apartment building on California Street.

A quick check of the tenant's registration had not turned up any Japanese names. He would send a couple of guys door to door in that building with a photo of the dead man for identity purposes.

Cooke would also have the detectives carry a police artist's sketch of Evans. Cooke picked up the phone and ordered up the artist. He could work with the artist himself, speeding up the process.

Then Cooke sat down, trying to figure who had leaked the address on Commercial Street. That was a leak he was going to have to plug.

Gavin felt good.

Dorn was gone, aboard a flight that would get him to Denver by dinnertime. Gavin was alone, the way it had to be. As he entered the thick San Francisco traffic he realized that it was his last night before going into action.

His hand tightened on the wheel. He needed a place to spend the night—preferably not a hotel. Gavin thought of Hillary Clarke, the redhead he'd surprised in Susan Billings's bathtub.

He had her address and phone number written on a piece of paper he'd stuffed in his inside coat pocket . . . he dug with his free hand, his fingers scissoring the paper neatly.

Her address was on California Street. Yes. He remembered. Near Golden Gate Park.

Gavin wondered if she would be glad to see him.

Scanlon was breathing hard.

The shovel had raised three blisters on his hands, one of which had already burst. He was panting, vapor pumping from his open mouth and his nostrils. It was cold and clammy in the hilly forest just off Inverness Ridge, fifty miles north of San Francisco, just past the Point Reyes Weather Station.

The miserable weather was just what the doctor ordered. Scanlon knew that a heavy fog was forecast, and later, strong winds.

Scanlon liked to be alone when he buried people.

He had slung her over his shoulder and trudged a hundred yards into the woods before allowing the deadweight to slip to the ground.

It had taken almost an hour to dig the grave.

Now he was ready.

He peeled away the blanket over Susan Billings's face. She appeared to be asleep, her mouth agape in the wonder of death. Scanlon rolled her into the grave with both hands.

He filled the grave, then tamped it down. Scanlon scattered leaves over the freshly turned earth, then pulled on his overcoat.

He straightened his tie as he walked back to his car.

twelve

Gavin worked the apartment buzzer for Hillary Clarke's second-story apartment. She answered over the speaker, her tone of voice clearly puzzled by Gavin's sudden visit.

She was standing in the doorway to her apartment when he cleared the second-floor landing. "What is it?" she said.

"Hillary," Gavin said, "you're a good friend of Susan's, aren't you?"

"Yes—of course."

"Then if you want to help her, you've got to help me. I need a place to stay for the night."

Her brow creased in a frown. "Is this some kind of ploy to get something else?"

"No," Gavin said. "I'm telling you the truth. I need a place to stay because the same people that kidnapped Susan are looking for me, and if they find me, they'll try to kill me."

"So you want to stay here. And if they find you here, they'll try to kill both of us?" She shook her head. "Why not stay at police headquarters?"

"Because I'm not a cop."

"But you told me—"

"No, I didn't. I didn't say I was a cop—you thought I was." Gavin shrugged. "I needed all the help I could get. I had to get you to talk."

She was skeptical. "And now you want to push in to my apartment and make yourself comfortable. Maybe even have me fix dinner—"

"Kind of you."

Hillary sighed. "I guess I just trust your face." She stepped aside and Gavin entered the small apartment. He walked to the living room windows that overlooked California Street. All was at peace in the world.

"Just who are you, anyway?" Hillary asked.

"My name's Evans," Gavin said. "Bob Evans. The man who was assaulted in Susan's apartment is a friend of mine. That's how I got involved."

Gavin walked to the window. Glancing down, he saw a dark blue Dodge pull up to the curb. Two men dressed in conservative tweed sport coats got out, checked the address, and walked to the apartment building's entrance.

"Have you found out anything about Susan? Is she all right?"

"I don't know," Gavin said. "The longer she's out there, the more dangerous it is for her."

Gavin wondered what the two cops wanted.

Hillary sighed again. "I wish there was something I could do to help," she said.

"You're helping right now," Gavin answered. "Tell you what—why don't you climb into the tub, have a nice hot bath, get all relaxed. I'll fix up something to eat while you're bathing. A nice quiet dinner for two."

Hillary's eyes brightened. "That's the best offer I've had in days," she said. She stood up. The bathroom was off the small hall that separated the living room and bedroom. "Say about thirty minutes?" she said.

"Perfect," Gavin answered, lighting a cigarette. When Hillary was in the bathroom, the water running, Gavin crossed the room to the kitchen area. Behind the counter Hillary had a bottle of Chivas Regal, a half-filled bottle of Tanqueray gin, and an almost-empty bottle of extra-dry vermouth.

He fished a few ice cubes from the freezer tray, stuck them in a long-stem water glass, then poured a double shot of Chivas.

He took off his coat, loosened his tie, then turned on the television. He wanted to look as natural as possible.

Gavin found a copy of that day's *Chronicle*. He settled down in the easy chair in front of the television, his eyes flicking from the printed page to the campy "Avengers" rerun on the tube.

It took about ten minutes for the detective to work his way to Hillary Clarke's apartment. When Gavin answered the door, he held the newspaper in one hand and his whiskey in the other. He looked like someone who'd just gotten home from the job, burned out, trying to relax.

"Yeah?"

"Detective O'Mire, San Francisco Police," The officer said. He was about Gavin's height, with the same coloring. The cop held up the photo of an Oriental. The man's eyes were open, but the opaque gaze and the lack of muscle tone in the facial muscles told Gavin it was a photo of a dead man.

"Ever seen this man?"

"No," Gavin said.

The cop then held up the police sketch of Gavin. It wasn't too bad, Gavin thought, though, like most police sketches, it wasn't close enough for most people to accurately I.D.

"What about him?" The cop asked.

Gavin looked at the sketch, then at the cop's face. "Looks a little like you," Gavin said.

The cop looked at the sketch. "Yeah. Well, here's my card"—he handed a plain business card to Gavin—"give us a call if you see this man, or if there's any suspicious activity."

"Will do," Gavin said.

The cop looked at his checklist. "You're H. Clarke, right?"

"Sure am," Gavin said. The cop nodded, moved off, and Gavin closed the door.

Gavin took his seat in front of the television, sipping his whiskey. He had had no idea the police had linked him up to this address. He had only been there once before. Apparently he'd been tailed, and not by the cops.

That meant they had probably picked him up when he left Susan Billings's apartment with Hillary Clarke. Gavin smiled. They were thorough bastards, all right.

"How's dinner coming?" Hillary Clarke's voice reached him from the bathtub.

"Relax," Gavin called back. He sipped whiskey as he stood in front of the open refrigerator, checking the stock.

There was a pound of ground round, plus assorted odds and ends.

Gavin hauled out the ground round and placed it on the counter. There were many ways to go. *Bifteck au roquefort* was one of his favorites, but a search revealed that Hillary Clarke did not stock Roquefort cheese;

bifteck à cheval lost out because 1) no eggs, 2) no butter. Gavin frowned. *Bifteck à l'anchois* would require anchovy paste, while *Bifteck hachés au gruyère* needed Gruyère cheese.

Bifteck au jambon was impossible without ham, and *Bifteck hachés à l'oignon* were never right if you substituted for the butter.

Gavin was going to settle for *Bifteck à la bordelaise*, even though it wasn't one of his favorites. But Hillary did have the necessary ingredients, the oil, onion, shallot, flour, red Bordeaux, salt, and pepper. The Bordeaux, while suspicious, would have to do.

Gavin dug a bag of frozen Garden Vegetables from the freezer and quickly prepared them for the stove, then pounded out patties of meat while the onion and shallot, chopped fine, sautéed in the skillet of heated oil. He added the meat patties, sprinkled with salt and pepper.

He refilled his glass with Chivas.

As soon as the meat was browned on one side Gavin turned the patties, then sprinkled them with flour. He poured in the wine and stirred, lowering the heat.

Gavin checked the vegetables and saw that they were about done. He got that together, finished his drink, and heated two plates under the broiler. As Hillary entered the living room, clad in an elegant black peignoir,

Gavin asked what she'd like to drink. It was going to be a good night.

"Scotch would be fine," she said. He prepared her drink and handed it to her. "What did you fix?" she asked, sniffing the air.

"You'll see," Gavin said. He got the plates under the broiler just in time. They cooled down a bit before he placed the beefsteaks on them, then poured the sauce over the meat, careful to strain the sauce with a spatula. He heaped the plates with vegetables, then carried the plates to the table.

"Oh," Hillary said. "Hamburgers."

"Colorado style," Gavin said.

During dinner they talked about the things that single people talk about when thrown together in such a situation. Gavin lied, and he assumed that Hillary did too. She was a charming woman, a trusting, generous, beautiful woman.

Hillary laughed.

"What's so funny?" Gavin asked. He smiled at her across the table. The lights were low, the music soft. He felt relaxed, well fed; so far, so good.

"Whiskey," Hillary said, holding up her glass. "I never drink whiskey with my meal."

"We should have had a nice red wine," Gavin said. "But sometimes a glass of whiskey goes with whatever you're eating."

She drained the glass. "Another?" she asked.

"It's your whiskey," Gavin said. He mixed two more drinks, humming a tune he had heard in France a few years before. He was not going to let reality rudely intrude into this special night.

Hillary's smile was a beacon as he returned to the small table. She accepted her glass, sipped, then said: "Just how did you get involved in this? I know what you told me about your friend and all that. But not many men carry things this far, even when their friends get hurt."

"I owe the man a lot."

Hillary smiled again. I'm getting sleepy," she said.

Hillary Clarke was a career woman in a town filled with career women. She was lonely, ripe for romance. Gavin put down his whiskey, realizing how alike the two of them were.

Later, when the full moon was visible from the bedroom window, Hillary was sound asleep in the large bed. Gavin, at the window in the light of the moon, his eyes puffy with sleepiness, his body still unable to let go.

thirteen

Gavin did a steady fifty-five south on Highway 101, planning to arrive in San Jose a few minutes before eleven. The morning was bright, the air crisp. Gavin was eager to play.

He had no clear idea of what awaited him at Electrotec, Inc., in San Jose. He had a gut feeling that it was a good place to poke his nose in. If he managed to spook someone, all the better. He wanted to put the birds in the air, outlined against a bright blue sky.

Gavin parked a few blocks from Electrotec. The Colorado plates on the Trans Am were not what he would have preferred, with half the police in Northern California looking for a male Coloradan. It was always the same. No deal that Gavin ever got into was ever completely squared off, every detail attended to. Most were lopsided, ragged actions that somehow worked.

The receptionist actually seemed glad to see him. She didn't know what he wanted, and didn't care. She was a beautiful brown-eyed Eurasian, apparently delighted with her good fortune in securing her present position.

Gavin gave her his business card, with the CBS logo and *"60 Minutes"* title suitably highlighted. Television's magic still worked; forty seconds later he was face to face with the head of Electrotec's Security—a Mr. Scanlon.

"What can we do for you?" Scanlon's manner had all the warmth of a pet rock. His smile was ever present, but Gavin picked up the other vibrations, the ones that enabled him to survive men like Scanlon.

"I'm an advance producer for the show. We're going to do a segment on security in the electronics industry. It's a follow-up on the Christopher Boyce story."

"I don't follow."

"Boyce was the man who walked away from TRW with damned near everything the government had in the way of intelligence secrets. According to Boyce, there was no security at TRW—that's how he was able to do it. Isn't NSA on the job? That's what my segment will be about."

Scanlon's forehead was peppered with sweat. Gavin hadn't expected to spook someone so quickly.

"What do you want from me?"

"A few minutes on camera, answering some questions on the recent upsurge in American technology being peddled to other nations like Russia, Israel, Japan."

"Do you have some I.D.?" Scanlon asked.

Gavin produced the AFTRA card, identifying him as a member in good standing.

Scanlon rubbed his palm against his jaw as he held the phony I.D. in his hand. "Can you wait a minute? I'll have to check this through."

Gavin smiled. "Go right ahead," He said.

As soon as Scanlon disappeared behind the security door Gavin turned, smiled at the delighted receptionist, and left the building.

He walked quickly to his car. He didn't need anything more from Scanlon. He had already seen enough.

He had seen that Electrotec was secured by early NSA alarm systems. There was a radio-wave alarm, activated when the waves are distorted by an intruder. Effective, damned near impossible to bypass.

That didn't matter.

The front door of Electrotec was enough to keep out most burglars, but Gavin had received special training in breaking and entering from the same people responsible for the design of that door: the National Security Agency, the government's largest and most powerful intelligence service, located in scenic Fort Meade, Maryland. Fort Meade was home to many of NSA's sixty thousand employees and was the place where all the intelligence it gathered was funneled.

Gavin drove north on Highway 101, towards San Francisco. He exited at Redwood City, midway to San Francisco. He booked a room for the night at a small motor court, neglected and forlorn, a good ten miles from the federal highway. The office window held a vacancy sign that had rusted in place.

Gavin paid in advance, declined to have a drink with the manager-owner, and retired to cabin 4, the Trans Am's Colorado plates still nibbling at his mind.

Scanlon was in shock.

What the hell was happening? There was no doubt in his mind that his visitor, bearing the phony CBS I.D., was the same bastard who'd been plaguing the operation almost from the beginning.

It was the man known as Evans. The man who had messed up Shigata's hit on Duffy in the hospital. The man they had tried to nail at Fisherman's Wharf, but missed.

The man should be lying low, waiting for the heat to blow over. He should be terrified by now, with all the firepower aimed at him.

But here he was, clowning around in the

lobby at Electrotec. What the hell was going on?

Scanlon considered his options. There weren't many. He was not going to call the police into it. He had, that morning, been visited by NSA agents, and those people weren't to be fooled with. They didn't abide by the legal technicalities, such as search warrants, cause for arrest, or any of it. If they smelled a rat they'd be all over Scanlon; he couldn't risk it.

He had to stay loose until Edwards made the connection. When the encryption device microcassette was delivered and payment was made, Scanlon wanted to be ready to accept his share.

His share amounted to all of it, of course. Edwards was merely a delivery boy, as far as Scanlon was concerned. He'd let Edwards think it was his idea, and he let Edwards think that Edwards would get the lion's share of the take.

Not so.

But that was of no consolation to Scanlon at the moment. Evans was loose, somewhere in the area, ready to muck up the operation.

Scanlon called in Taylor, Carson, and Bell. The three uniformed security men were used to doing special work for Scanlon. He had made sure of that before he hired them at Electrotec.

"I want you three on immediate twenty-four-hour standby," he said. "Taylor, Carson—you two move in to Bell's apartment and stay by the phone. I might need you. This operation will be plainclothes. Bring your weapons. That's all."

The three ex-mercenaries could be trusted to do exactly as he told them.

Scanlon longed for the opportunity to turn them loose on the gray-eyed joker who was causing him so much concern.

It would be the high point of the operation, Scanlon thought. Delicious.

Jimmy Shigata took another pain pill. The hot throbbing in his finger was worse. He looked at the bandaged stump and felt his stomach turn. The thought of disfigurement had always frightened him. The reality of it disgusted him.

What had started out as a career step up had turned into a nightmare. He had been supplying girls to the Tokyo organization for over two years, and there had never been any complaints.

His pose as a talent agent was still effective. Los Angeles was stocked with beautiful girls quite willing to believe that he represented show business interests in the Orient, and that a trip to Japan was just the thing for them.

So when the organization approached him and asked him to oversee a special job for a special girl, he quickly agreed. After all, the organization had been good to Shigata, and he wanted to keep them happy.

Now he was ass-deep in murder; he hadn't counted on that. Mr. Oki had exposed Shigata, without telling Shigata exactly what was going on. It was obvious now that the Billings woman was not being kidnapped merely to send her into prostitution. She was the cog in a machine already out of control.

The machine was killing people, and if Shigata wasn't careful, it was going to kill him too. It was no longer a simple matter of putting girls on airplanes, dreams of fame and glory gleaming in their eyes. His angry stump reminded him that there was no room for mistakes.

He was riding in the rear of a fully equipped Dodge van. There were four of them riding with Shigata. Two were up front, enjoying the drive. The other two were playing cards in the rear. They had their shirts off. Their torsos were covered with intricate oriental tattoos.

The *yakuza* were on a mission of honor to avenge the deaths of their mates. Shigata was only anxious to get it over with.

It had been made clear to Shigata this time. There were to be no more reprimands, no more trivial punishments. If he failed again, the *yakuza* would execute him.

Shigata wiggled his stumb and felt the pain all the way to his elbow.

Scanlon finished dinner in the small French restaurant, then had two cups of coffee before setting out for his apartment. He bought a copy of *Hustler* at the all-night newsstand. Scanlon liked the magazine's blend of sex and violence. By the time he arrived at his apartment it was already ten minutes past seven.

A terminal had been installed in Scanlon's living room. With it, the electronic security gear at Electrotec could be controlled. He checked the display and saw that everything was normal. He sat down, activated the keyboard, and punched in the evening's instructions.

Scanlon liked working with computers; but they were toys to him, superintelligent objects that he didn't understand. Television, he thought. It's all television.

Scanlon sat back in the typing chair. The screen acknowledged his instructions; Scanlon hit another key. He waited thirty seconds, then pushed in another command. The screen filled with a view of an empty corridor. Scanlon smiled. The killer was up and functioning, the robot's TV camera allowing Scanlon to see through the robot's eye.

It was just another toy, but a highly deadly one. Scanlon wondered if he'd ever have another chance to see the robot in action. Now *that* would be a sight.

Gavin drove past Electrotec twice before parking on the side street. It was quiet. Nothing is more deserted than a business zone in California after working hours.

Gavin figured that he'd be tripping alarms as soon as he went through the front door.

That was OK.

The security systems used by government contractors were sensitive—too sensitive. For every genuine burglary that they detected, they detected a few dozen nonburglaries, causing security patrols to be hesitant about answering every alarm.

It was SOP for most security people to double-check any alarm, on the excellent grounds that most alarms were nothing at all, just the software or the hardware malfunctioning. Usually someone had to check it out before the police could be notified. The police had also answered too many phony alarms, and were not eager to go into high gear at every reported break-in.

Gavin figured that even with the alarms going off as soon as he entered, he'd have thirty minutes or so before anyone got there—anyone that he'd have to worry about.

Not that he planned to stay inside thirty minutes. All he wanted to do was make a mess, let them know that he'd been there. Like fox droppings in the hen house—just enough to make the farmer crazy.

Gavin made his entry through a side door that presented even less of a challenge than the front door, and had the added virtue of being recessed in a dark doorway.

Once inside, Gavin felt his heart pumping with adrenaline, his mind clear and his senses, steady.

He tried a door that opened on a white corridor.

It was very quiet.

fourteen

The high winds had blown the fog south of Inverness Ridge. Pete Nelson stood gazing at the stars, bright and piercing in the chill evening air.

He still had a two-hour hike before he reached his favorite campground. Pete had gotten hung up in San Francisco traffic and didn't cross into Marin County as early as he had thought he would. The hike wasn't anything special, but he would have preferred to do it during the daylight hours.

Still, it was a sharp pleasure to be heading into the woods below Inverness Ridge, the only man for miles around, snug and warm in his hiking gear.

The heavy winds had disturbed things, piling leaves in uneven clumps, in spots even clearing the forest floor. He saw the mound at once, bare and painful as a scraped knee. It was the size and shape of a grave.

Pete Nelson had to dig for less than ten minutes.

The alarm sounded in Scanlon's apartment. He crushed out the cigarette and flipped his copy of *Hustler* onto the coffee table.

That alarm was the robot's alarm.

Scanlon flicked the keyboard as he sat down at the console. The camera, located in the robot's head, sent images of the hall leading to Clayton Edward's office.

The door to the office stood open. Scanlon fed the robot the command to obey its heat-seeking guidance system. The body temperature of a human being was the number the robot liked best of all.

Scanlon picked up the telephone. Carson answered on the first ring, and Scanlon told him to get over to Electrotec, along with Taylor and Bell.

Scanlon didn't have to go into details.

Gavin had been surprised to discover that Electrotec didn't even have a watchman. The building was secured only by its electronic systems. Gavin thought such a security policy was a shortsighted one.

He had worked his way down the hall,

visited several offices, overturned a few wastebaskets, ransacked two or three desks.

He was in the office of the company's president, Clayton Edwards.

Gavin found nothing of any interest whatsoever.

He felt satisfied, however. There would be no question that someone had been there, and that was what Gavin wanted. He wanted to rattle them bad enough so that they'd make a move. Gavin needed to track, not be tracked.

Gavin heard the whirring sound in the hall outside the office. He frowned. Cleaning lady? He stepped quietly to the open door, then peered into the hall.

The damned thing was a little over six feet tall, roughly humanoid in appearance, though it had no discernible legs. It glided towards him, its metal arms extending the width of the hall.

There was no getting past it.

Damn! Gavin disliked dealing with machinery that was aimed at him. He had found that all the qualities that made him a survivor were as nothing to a machine. Machines versus meat were contests that were all too predictable.

He had already been inside a touch too long. He was now on his own time, and he didn't like it. No matter how sloppy security was, someone would show up sooner or later.

And until then he had a steel monster in the hall, set on KILL.

He slammed shut the heavy wood door, then realized that there was no lock on it. As he backed across the room he saw the doorknob turn, then the door open.

In the doorway stood the machine.

Scanlon grinned.

The guy didn't look so cocky on television. Of course, looking at that damned robot coming at you was enough to make any man a little nervous.

Scanlon decided to make him sweat. He set the robot in a stationary mode, guarding the door. There was no other way for him to get out of the room.

Scanlon saw that the man was inspecting the robot from behind Clayton Edwards's desk. He wasn't dumb enough to try for the door. He knew enough about those steel arms to know what they could do.

Scanlon checked his watch. Taylor, Carson, and Bell should be there any moment. It felt good having this guy pinned down like a bug.

Scanlon was going to have a lot fun with him, whoever he was. Scanlon liked to make people talk, and it had been a while since he'd had the chance.

Besides, he always enjoyed the drive to Inverness Ridge.

* * *

Gavin heard them coming down the hall.

He was still standing behind the desk. There was no suitable cover in the room, unless the men were armed with BB guns. He had the Walther snug under his arm, but now didn't seem the time for it.

The first man to the door shoved his .45 past the robot's metallic bulk and grinned at Gavin. "Hello, asshole," the blond man said.

There were two others. While the blond surfer type held Gavin under the sway of the .45, one of them flicked off a control device mounted on the robot's back. The machine was now lifeless. They wheeled it out of the way, then came into the office.

The Surfer was still grinning. He wore a down vest, jeans, and desert boots. The other two were about the same age—early thirties, Gavin judged—and the same style. One wore a PeterBilt cap, the other was balding.

"Call Scanlon," the Surfer said. "What the hell are we supposed to do now?"

"Didn't he tell you?" asked the man wearing the PeterBilt cap.

"Hell no. Never does. Just says, go there, do that—you know, he likes to run things, man. C'mon. Call the dude. I don't want to spend the whole damned night with this guy."

When they got Scanlon on the phone his instructions were short and to the point.

"Scanlon says we should kick him around till he tells us where he left his car."

"What if I didn't bring a car?" Gavin asked. He felt better when he spoke.

"If you didn't, you're in for one hell of a beating," PeterBilt said, smashing his fist into his hand.

The Surfer was getting angry. "A car? What the hell's all this about a car, for chrissakes?"

"Scanlon wants us to bring the car along. He doesn't want any sign of this guy around by morning." He turned to the third man. "You got to stay here and clean up after this asshole. Straighten up, then meet us back at Bell's."

The balding man nodded.

"Now about the car . . ."

"Let's save time," Gavin said. "You guys don't want to have to carry me, do you? Why not let me take you right to it. It's just around the corner."

PeterBilt laughed. "Scanlon said he'd do that," PeterBilt said. "Said the guy was a stone chickenshit dude. Let's kick his ass anyway."

"Hold it," said the Surfer. He didn't want to get mixed up in anything, if he could help it. "Check him out for a piece, and lets get the hell out of here."

PeterBilt found the Walther immediately. He jerked it from the holster and turned it in his hands. "Nasty-lookin' thing," he said, eyeing the Walther. Then his eyes met Gavin's. "You know how to use somethin' like this?"

"Can it," said the Surfer. "Let's get the fuck outta here. Now!"

The Surfer walked behind Gavin down the hall and out the front door. There was a Volvo station wagon there, and the Surfer told Gavin to get in.

"Where's the car?" He asked. Gavin was in the backseat. The Surfer was driving. PeterBilt, in the front passenger seat, was turned, pointing the .45 at Gavin's midsection.

When they arrived at the Trans Am, the Surfer parked and locked the Volvo. 'We'll come back for it later," he said to PeterBilt. "Get in there and check it out. He might have another piece real handy."

PeterBilt found nothing. He checked under the dash, along the seats, the glove compartment, and the side panels. He did not find the release button for the console lid.

"Clean," he said.

"In the back," the Surfer said, shoving the .45 into Gavin's kidney.

Gavin sat in the back, his throbbing kidney a constant reminder that this was the original no-bullshit deal. He was alive only because they had some other use for him, and when that was over, he would be dead—if he let them.

"You know the way to Scanlon's?" the Surfer asked.

"Sure," replied PeterBilt.

"Then you drive. I'm going to keep an eye on this guy. I don't want nothin' goin' wrong."

As they drove towards the southeast suburbs of San Jose, PeterBilt was laughing. "Ain't that Taylor somethin'? Scanlon wants the place cleaned up and we lay it right in Taylor's lap. I wonder if that clown'll ever figure out he gets all the shitwork?"

The Surfer's eyes were on Gavin. He wasn't laughing. He was nervous, anxious to get his end of the operation over with. He grinned suddenly at Gavin. "What'd you think when you saw that goddamn robot?"

"Bad drugs," said Gavin.

"Real bad. That damned thing would've made you a whole new frame," the Surfer said. "Put your ass where your elbow is, that damned thing would. Good thing for you you kept outta that thing's way."

PeterBilt was laughing again. "For a little while, anyway."

Inspector Dan Cooke saw them coming down the hall. Simpson was the first one into Cooke's office, and he did the talking while Curry slumped in a straight-back chair, making it look like it hurt.

"So she's dead," Simpson said.

Cooke nodded. "They dug her up earlier this evening. The guy buried her good and proper, but we got lucky. She was O.D.ed, probably within the past twenty-four hours."

All the tension was gone from Curry's face. It was as if someone had opened a valve in the bottom of his foot and all his energy had leaked out. He looked ten years older than the last time Cooke had seen him.

"So we're on our way to Washington," Simpson said. "Cat's out of the bag now."

"We've still got a kidnapper out there—a murderer."

Curry looked up. "That's your problem," he said. "It doesn't concern us. Susan Billings is dead, and that probably means that the situation is already compromised."

"Compromised?"

"They got what they wanted from her," Curry explained, "then they killed her. "This is not going to go down well in Washington."

fifteen

Clayton Edwards was a happy man.

He admired his trim figure in the full-length mirror suspended behind his bedroom door. Flat stomach, good muscle tone. He had taken good care of his body.

Twenty-four hours away from enough money to go where he wanted, to do what he chose. He felt a semisexual excitement in his loins. It was a chance for a new life, a chance most men never got.

All he had to do was fly to Los Angeles, turn over the microcassette to Oki, and he'd be home free.

The thought of all that cash thrilled him. Of course, he'd have to deal with Scanlon, but that would be handled from a distance. He didn't trust Scanlon. The man was a sociopath; his mind didn't operate along the usual lines. Scanlon would kill him without a thought and Clayton Edwards knew it.

Clayton Edwards wasn't going to give Scanlon the chance.

The microcassette was carefully tucked into the inside pocket of his herringbone sport coat. He would pack it later. He smiled. The ease of the operation was truly astonishing. Clayton Edwards had had his nervous moments, but everything was now working perfectly.

The girl was dead—that was a shame. Still, Scanlon had been correct in his appraisal of the situation. Alive, she was a potential hazard. She knew Scanlon, and that was a direct link to Clayton Edwards.

Scanlon had been correct in his assessment of the National Security Agency's reaction to Billings's abduction. They had assumed that she was kidnapped in order to force her to divulge the secrets of the new encryption device. It was like waving a cape at a charging bull—NSA never looked behind the flimsy lure.

Clayton Edwards glanced at the electronic alarm clock on the night table beside his bed. He was going to get a good night's sleep—he wanted to be fresh, clear headed, in the morning. He hated Los Angeles, but for $750,000, he would go anywhere.

What had he been so nervous about? After all, it was all so incredibly easy!

The Surfer kept the .45 positioned perfectly as Gavin climbed out of the car. He knew what he was doing. There was no chance for Gavin to go for the Uzi tucked in the console. That was OK. He needed information, and the Surfer and PeterBilt would lead him to it.

Scanlon lived in a modern apartment complex especially designed for lonely single people with delusions of grandeur. Total security prevailed at the main gate—a buzzer-switch opened the wire-mesh door.

Once past the main gate the Surfer tucked the .45 behind his down vest. It was still in his hand, and Gavin had no ideas of testing the Surfer's reaction time to any sudden moves.

They walked past the billiard–table tennis room, occupied by two middle-aged men huffing and puffing through what must have been an all-night Ping-Pong match. They weren't noticed as they crossed the poolside area, deserted in the chill evening air.

Scanlon's apartment was a ground-floor unit that stood twenty yards from the pool.

Scanlon opened the door and they entered. "Well, well," Scanlon said as he closed the door. His eyes had a reddish hue that gave him a drugged appearance. "Mr. CBS. Mr. Sixty Minutes. I'm glad to see you again," Scanlon said.

"The pleasure's all yours," Gavin answered.

The apartment was furnished in a heavy, suffocating style, drapes, carpets, and thick soft furniture giving the place the feel of a sensory-deprivation tank. There was too much pink. Gavin frowned. The place might have been furnished by a middle-aged spinster on terminal dollhouse burnout.

The Surfer jabbed Gavin with the .45, moving him forward a few steps. "What now?" The Surfer asked Scanlon.

"You boys are in luck," Scanlon said. "At first I figured I was going to have to saddle you with some dirty work tonight—but I just heard from some boys who're only too happy to take care of this little mess." Scanlon turned to Gavin. "You remember those boys—they tried to introduce themselves at the video arcade." He shook his head. "Damned unfriendly of you to trash them that way. Those Japanese, they got a long memory, and they got a real hard-on for you." He grinned. "Especially Shigata."

"Let me get this straight," Gavin said. "Susan Billings was taken to make it look like she was the centerpiece of this deal. But you're the one that's tied in with the *yakuza*, and they're going to buy Susan Billings's research from you."

Scanlon grinned. "More or less. I'll tell you something else too, dirtbag. Tomorrow's the day. You'll be face down in a ditch somewhere by then. You know how nasty those *yakuza* can be. I'll be thinking of you. You know why?" Scanlon's smile was gone—a teeth-baring snarl of anger had taken over. "Because you almost made this deal take a shit, my friend. Almost. Not quite." He slapped Gavin across the face, his ring opening Gavin's cheek.

"Somehow I don't see the *yakuza* dealing with a guy like you," Gavin said. Scanlon's eyes narrowed. Gavin decided to push it. "You're too dangerous. Too messy. You don't have the contacts. You wouldn't know who to sell technology to. You wouldn't recognize an encryption device if it bit you on the ass."

Scanlon's face was scarlet with anger. He didn't like to appear weak in front of his goons. Gavin had known plenty of guys just like Scanlon. Push the right button, then stand back. They'd tell you all you needed to know.

"You're a dead man," Scanlon said.

Gavin laughed at him. "Maybe. But you won't kill me here. Are you going to carry my body out of here wrapped in a leaky blanket? What if someone notices? Then the whole deal's gone, and you'll wind up in the joint with your head in a toilet bowl and a string of cons lined up behind you working out their sex lives."

Scanlon's color had risen another notch or two. He looked like he was going to explode. The Surfer was smiling and PeterBilt was open mouthed. Scanlon was losing his authority damned fast—he was going to have to do something.

"I wish I could handle you myself," Scanlon whispered, and a shudder almost escaped from Gavin. Scanlon was scary, like all psychos.

"Yeah, sure," Gavin yawned. "But you'll be busy looking for the guy who's supposed to pay you off. I bet you'll be looking for a long time too."

Scanlon wanted to kill him on the spot. But that would be stupid, and he knew it. Shigata would arrive soon; Shigata would handle it.

Jimmy Shigata made the call collect because he didn't have the right change. "Mr. Oki? I know that your instructions were real plain, but something's come up I think you should know about."

Oki told him to explain it quickly.

"This guy we've been after—alll of a sudden he turns up in Scanlon's apartment," Shigata said quickly. "It's too neat, too tied together."

Oki asked Shigata what he thought they should do.

"Scanlon wants me to burn him," Shigata said. "And I will if you want me to. But what if there's some game going on here?"

Oki saw the point at once. He told Shigata to corral the mysterious stranger and bring him to Los Angeles.

Mr. Oki would settle the mystery once and for all.

Shigata climbed inside the van and gave the driver directions to Scanlon's. Scanlon was a sleazeball. That much Shigata knew. He didn't trust him. He wasn't going to follow his orders blindly either. Let Oki decide what to do. That way there would be no recriminations, no blame to suddenly fall on Shigata's thin shoulders.

He told the driver to hurry up.

It had felt good to mock Scanlon in front of his men. Now that it was over and Gavin was still alive, he was glad that he had done it. Scanlon could have lost control and blown him away, but he hadn't.

Gavin had judged the situation correctly.

It boosted his confidence. It gave him hope in his present situation.

He was in the back of the van, in the right rear corner. Shigata and one of the nameless *yakuza* watched him. Gavin was staring at the weapons they held: two .44 Magnums. That firepower was enough for Gavin. There was no getting out of the van, and there was no room for dumb moves.

He was in for the night. Six or seven hours to drive to Los Angeles—that was going to be a long time to spend looking down the barrels. "Hey," Gavin said. "I've got an idea."

Shigata ran the Magnum to single action. "Shut up."

Gavin almost laughed in his face. They might try to kill him if he tried something physical—but their intent was to get him to Los Angeles alive. Talking was OK.

"Tell the driver to stop at the next all-night market," Gavin said. "Buy me a bottle of Scotch. I'll sleep all night and you two guys can relax."

Shigata licked his lips. Gavin thought that Shigata looked like he could use a drink himself. Gavin counted on the assumption that Shigata was the only one of his captors who spoke English. If one of the others understood what had been said, Shigata would be forced to deny Gavin, in order to save face.

Shigata thought it over for a moment, then caught Gavin's eye. Staring at Gavin, Shigata said something in Japanese to the driver, who grunted a reply.

Fifteen minutes later Gavin had a bottle of Scoresby's in his hand. A sip told him that Scoresby's was a fine Scotch for the price.

Gavin took another sip. He thought about what was coming up for him. A meeting somewhere, then a quick word to Shigata followed by a drive to some deserted spot where Gavin would take a round behind the ear.

The old Gavin wouldn't have gotten into this position. The old Gavin, remorselessly efficient, would never have been taken. Never. PeterBilt and the Surfer would have been stiched with the Uzi, if Gavin had allowed things to get that far.

But the old Gavin was a businessman, a professional who did the best job with the cards that were dealt to him. There were no personal motives in the affairs of a terminator. Just jobs, one after the other. That was why he had stopped.

And now he was into it all the way, and it was out of control. He was an amateur at this—what the hell did he know about investigating? Nothing. He had been following his nose. He took a deep drink from the bottle and welcomed the expanding, false, sense of security.

"Wake me for breakfast," Gavin said, stretching out on the carpeted deck of the van. Shigata's eyes looked dead to Gavin. Shigata tracked him carefully, the Magnum a third, dead eye.

sixteen

PSA is the commuter airline connecting various California cities. It prides itself on friendly service and reasonable prices. There is no first class on PSA—it is all coach.

Clayton Edwards squirmed as Scanlon settled into the seat next to him. "This is going to be a good day," Scanlon said, flashing his most sincere smile at Edwards.

As much as Edwards hated to admit it, he agreed with Scanlon. In a few hours he would hand over the microcassette that contained the plans for the VLSI, the Very Large Scale Integration circuit, the Array Processing Encryption Device. Edwards like to roll through the technological litany, playing with the words, an executive on top of his craft.

Edwards felt so good that, for a moment, an almost friendly feeling enveloped him. Scanlon, seated next to him, became the object of Edwards's good-feelings. "We made it," Edwards said, his eyes shining. "Home free."

Scanlon's eyes danced with homicidal glee. Edwards was going to be easy. He was so caught up in the completion of the deal that he was going to get careless, and then Scanlon would take him off.

"Yeah," Scanlon answered, grinning. "We made it. All the way. No loose strings. None."

That sobered up Edwards. "Even that," Edwards said. "You've been very thorough."

Scanlon nodded. "The only way to be. No one around to tie me or you to anything."

It was not the first time that Edwards had noticed the predatory look in Scanlon's eyes.

Gavin awoke with the sound of freeway traffic in his ears. He sat up, fumbled in his shirt pocket for a cigarette. Shigata was talking to the driver. The other *yakuza* held Gavin under the gaze of a .44 Magnum.

Shigata turned around. He grinned at Gavin. "Ten minutes to go, champ."

Gavin nodded. "What's the point? Why the trip to L.A.?"

"I'm just takin' care of business," Shigata said. "No mistakes. Not for me."

Gavin eyed the bandage over Shigata's stump. "Got a light?" Gavin said. Shigata tossed him a book of matches. Gavin fired the Marlboro, inhaled, then sat back as he blew a cone of smoke.

The bottle was still over half full; Gavin hit it once to wake up.

They were off the freeway now, winding downhill. Gavin remembered that Little Tokyo was located in downtown Los Angeles, near Chinatown and Olvera Street. Gavin grinned. Just because his abductors were Japanese, he assumed they were taking him to Little Tokyo! Totally stereotyped thinking. Headquarters was probably a Spanish bungalow in Beverly Hills, Cocaine Consumption Capital of the Western World.

"Where are we headed?" Gavin asked.

"Little Tokyo," Shigata said. "Where else?"

Gavin was suddenly depressed. What the hell had gone wrong? He had been leading a peaceful, uneventful, pleasant life. Then a friend got hurt and Gavin tried to find out why. Now he was in the back of a van with two hostile .44s. If everything worked out, he would still be alive tomorrow. If not . . .

Mr. Oki checked his wristwatch, his impatience evident to the other men in the room. They were gathered in a conference room on the second floor of the Lotus, a Japanese restaurant just inside Little Tokyo, in downtown Los Angeles.

They were seated at a rectangular conference table decorated with pots of coffee and tea. Half-filled cups and overflowing ashtrays testified to the group's anxiety.

Shigata was due with the American who had almost single-handedly brought the operation to an unfortunate end. Oki smiled. It would be good to meet such a man face to face. He had proven to be a worthy opponent.

It would also be interesting to watch Scanlon and Edwards for any signs of treachery when they are confronted with the American. It was good of Shigata to alert Oki to the possibility of treachery. It was good that Shigata did not kill the American as Scanlon ordered. It was good that Shigata was finally thinking. Oki knew that the loss of a finger often improves a man's thinking processes. Such had been the case with Shigata.

The men grouped around the table were *yakuza*, anxious that the transfer happen. Their organization was to be well paid for its participation, but there were other benefits as well. As Japanese, they were always ready to advance the National Interest. It was for this reason that the *yakuza* were accepted in Japan. Whatever their dealings, they were always Japanese first, and that was what mattered.

There were four of them with Mr. Oki, their conversation mostly whispered. There was a knock on the door and one of them quickly answered it. "They have arrived," a waiter from the restaurant downstairs reported.

Oki checked his wristwatch again. Right on time. Shigata was to be commended for this operation. Perhaps there was a place for the young man in Mr. Oki's far-flung empire. A bit of seasoning in Manila, then on to Tokyo, Hong Kong. With his knowledge of English, Shigata would do well in Mr. Oki's European offices.

Mr. Oki could hear them on the landing outside the door. The American was the first one into the room, looking rumpled, unclean—Mr. Oki's nose flared in distaste. True, the American had spent an uncomfortable night at gunpoint. Still, he should take more care with his appearance.

The American was tall by Japanese standards, perhaps six feet in height. He was trim through the torso but moved quickly and easily. A dangerous man. His clear gray eyes seemed to mock Mr. Oki as the American's gaze traveled the room.

"So this is it," the American said. His eyes locked with Mr. Oki's. "And you're Mister Big."

"Mister Big?" Oki's confusion was instant and the mocking grin of the American infuriated him. "Do not say stupidities to me," Mr. Oki growled. He nodded to the *yakuza* standing beside the American and grinned with pleasure when the *yakuza*'s balled fist thudded into the American's back, at the kidney level.

The American staggered to a chair and was forced down in it by another *yakuza*. "Immobilize him," Mr. Oki ordered, and within moments Gavin's wrists and ankles were secured to the chair. He was breathing hard, the pain in his back finally easing off.

"Who are you?" Mr. Oki asked.

"A friend of the man that was left for dead in the girl's apartment," Gavin said.

"Do you take me for a fool? A friend? Which organization are you with?"

Gavin shook his head. "No organization," Gavin said.

Mr. Oki stepped close to Gavin and slapped him twice, hard. The blows brought the blood to Gavin's face and his eyes locked on Oki again.

There was another knock on the conference room door. The others had arrived.

Mr. Oki stepped back and smiled with satisfaction. "This will be enjoyable," he said in English.

Gavin said nothing.

The Japanese was right about one thing, Gavin realized as soon as Scanlon and the other man walked into the room. The look on Scanlon's face when he saw Gavin almost made the drive to Los Angeles worthwhile.

"What the hell!" Scanlon reached inside his jacket, but his arms were pinned from behind by one of Jimmy Shigata's *yakuza*.

"Relax," Shigata said. "He ain't goin' anywhere."

Scanlon's face was crimson. "He's supposed to be dead!" he yelled. Scanlon turned to Edwards. "I don't know what the hell is going on!"

Mr. Oki stepped forward. "So you are Clayton Edwards," he said, extending his hand. Edwards had to drag his eyes from the sight of Gavin, tied up, grinning at him.

"Yes. Yes. I have the microcassette."

"Very good," Mr. Oki said. He indicated that Scanlon and Edwards take chairs at the conference table. Mr. Oki placed an attaché case on the table and worked the combination. Then he opened the lid, revealing symmetrical stacks of one-hundred dollar bills. Gavin calculated as quickly as possible. The stacks appeared to be thick enough to be worth twenty thousand dollars apiece, and if there were double the number of stacks visible to him—he counted eleven stacks, with room for one more—the case held roughly a quarter of a million in each layer of stacked bills. The total for the case could be a half million, or as high as three-quarters of a million if they were triple-stacked.

Edwards handed over the cassette. Mr. Oki handed it to a *yakuza*, who took it to the open door leading to the computer room. There it would be verified as quickly as possible.

Gavin's eyes caught Edwards. "Where's the girl?" Gavin asked.

Edwards blanched. Scanlon cut in, his thin lips pulled back in a grin. "She's junk," Scanlon said. "The same's you're gonna be."

"You did it yourself?" Gavin's voice conveyed little more than bland curiosity of it all.

Scanlon nodded, his arms folded across his thick chest. "I'd like to do you too. Maybe I will."

"Sure you will. You'll leave Edwards alone with all that money just for the pleasure of twisting me off. And when you're done, all you'll have to do is find him to get your share."

"I'll take my share right now!" Scanlon said. "Then you and me can settle up."

Edwards was not taking it well. "We can't divide the money now," he whispered. "For God's sake—don't panic now. Let's do as we planned. Return to San Jose. Carry this off the right way!"

Scanlon was considering Edwards. "Yeah?

Then let's say I carry the money. Any objections?"

Oki's amused expression irritated Scanlon. "You think this is funny?" Scanlon's eyes were bugging. He was losing control quickly. Gavin was glad to see it happen. He hoped one of the *yakuza* would behead Scanlon.

Scanlon struggled in the *yakuza*'s strong arms, but it was useless. Scanlon's holster was emptied of his .45 automatic by another *yakuza*.

It was finally dawning on Scanlon. "What the hell's goin' on?" He asked.

Edwards stood to leave. "I still don't understand why he's here," Edwards said, indicating Gavin.

Mr. Oki shrugged. "An indulgence," he answered. "A test of some sort? In any case, he will join Mr. Scanlon in a final passage."

Scanlon looked at Gavin.

Gavin smiled at him.

Then Scanlon tried to break free from the restraining hands and was stopped by a short stroke to the base of the skull delivered with the butt of his own .45 automatic.

Edwards looked once at Gavin, then picked up the attaché case.

Jimmy Shigata was breathing hard. He knew what was next and he was priming himself for the job. "Take them," Mr. Oki said, and as soon as the words were out of his mouth, Shigata swung into action.

"Wrap that clown up," Shigata said, pointing to Scanlon. "You—any trouble and you go down too."

Gavin nodded his head. "I wouldn't want to miss a moment of it," he said.

Edwards, clutching the cash-packed attaché case to his chest, took a final look at Scanlon. The red-haired Scanlon glared back, his eyes filled with kill lust.

"We needed someone," Clayton Edwards said.

"What?" Scanlon snapped. Gavin was amazed at the amount of fight left in Scanlon after taking the skull smack from the butt of the automatic.

"We needed someone they could have," Edwards said. "We have to throw someone to the wolves, Scanlon. When it's over, the police will know that you kidnapped Susan Billings, that you killed her, and that you killed the NSA agent who was watching her apartment."

Scanlon sneered. "How?"

"Meehan," Edwards said. "Meehan's our man, not yours. He's going to be in a position, with the evidence we give him, to convince everyone that you were the man responsible. Of course you'll be dead by then, a victim of the people you were dealing with."

Scanlon made as if to rise, but he was batted down harshly by the *yakuza* behind him. Gavin shifted in his chair. Even though Scanlon was a complete and total scumbag, he was no worse than the carefully coiffed, well-dressed Clayton Edwards, who would probably pass out at the sight of blood. Scanlon had been played for a sucker and that was too bad—for Scanlon. It didn't matter a bit to Gavin. Gavin was looking at all the men in the room with the eyes of an executioner, bland, unconcerned, yet aware of every rippling detail.

Mr. Oki was suddenly all business. "You must move quickly," he hissed to Shigata. Jimmy Shigata nodded, shoved his pistol into his waistband, and then directed his men to pack up Scanlon and Gavin.

Freed of his bonds, Gavin rubbed his forearms, restoring circulation. Mr. Oki stood quietly, watching. In his hand was the microcassette.

"That little thing's pretty damned valuable. But is it worth all those lives?" Gavin asked.

Mr. Oki's eyes danced with amusement. "With the data contained here, a device can be constructed that will control the security of information for banking systems, for governments, for military operations. That is power. In this case, power for sale. There are already several bidders. It will be most interesting to see who wins out."

Scanlon made one more attempt to break free of the arms restraining him. He was slugged twice with a .45 automatic, and he sagged to the floor like a dead man. Gavin watched it. He saw the sadistic grin on Shigata's face as he slid the .45 back into his waistband. "Load him in the van!" Shigata ordered.

As Scanlon was carried from the room, Gavin said, "You're pretty good with that."

Shigata grinned again. "You're gonna find out just how good," he said.

They left by the rear stairway, which led to the alley.

Scanlon had been pitched into the van. A *yakuza* holding a .44 Magnum had climbed in after Scanlon, pulling the doors closed behind him.

The van had left Little Tokyo immediately, followed by Gavin's '74 Trans Am. "We want them to find the car with you and Scanlon," Shigata had said. "We want it all tied up and clean. Nothing missing. Cops love that."

Gavin had sat in the backseat with Shigata riding shotgun. Jimmy Shigata was half turned in his seat, his left arm along the backrest, his right hand held low, the .45 directed at Gavin's midsection.

Under Shigata's right hand was the console.

Gavin stared straight ahead, watching the van sway in the sudden gusts of wind buffeting the northbound freeway traffic. Griffith Park was on Gavin's left. The right-turn indicator of the van suddenly started blinking and the Trans Am followed, easing over into the exit lane.

There were plenty of deserted spots in Griffith Park.

seventeen

After a long hot summer Los Angeles always tries to burn down. The dry chaparral on the hillsides was brown, ready to burn.

The access road to the hillside trails was closed because of the fire danger, something Shigata hadn't figured on. They drove through the winding lanes that crisscrossed Griffith Park, looking for a killing ground.

It was hopeless. They were going to have to park, then walk in. Gavin was cheered. Things were beginning to break his way.

The van stopped and the Trans Am pulled in behind it. Fifty yards away, on a green plain of gently rolling grass, a few families had settled in for a picnic. The van and the Trans Am were parked on the road's edge. A short walk would take them over the hill, and Gavin had no doubt that Shigata had brought a silencer with him.

The van's doors opened and Scanlon, bloody and groggy, was being helped out. Shigata stepped out of the Trans Am and the driver, already out, hurried to help the other *yakuza*, supporting Scanlon.

The .45 in Shigata's hand was covered by a satin jacket draped over his forearm. "Just take it easy," Shigata said. "Don't make me rush."

Gavin leaned forward, his left hand searching for the control that would pop the console lid. As he pushed the seat forward his hand found the recessed button.

Gavin pushed it.

Shigata had glanced at Scanlon, wobbly between two *yakuza*. Gavin reached into the console, gripped the Uzi, taking off the safety.

Shigata heard the mechanical noise and spun around, his expression a cross between fear and surprise. Gavin loosed a short burst that exploded Shigata's chest and tore off a chunk of his shoulder. Shigata popped backwards, landing flat on his back.

Gavin was out of the Trans Am, rolling on the sharp gravel that bordered the lane. Scanlon was slowly sinking to the ground, deserted by the two *yakuza* who had been supporting him.

Gavin cut them down as they ran for cover, stiching them across the back, then rolling again as the fourth *yakuza* cut loose with the

Magnum. Gavin felt the concussion from the round as it tore into the ground to his right, then he was on his knees walking a pattern of fire into the *yakuza*'s face. The *yakuza* was punched with the force of a dozen rounds, ending up in a crumpled heap beside the van's right rear tire.

Scanlon had taken advantage of the action to crawl towards one of the dead *yakuza*. As Gavin spun around he saw that Scanlon had picked up the .44 that had fallen to the ground and was lying prone, squeezing of a round in Gavin's direction. The round collapsed the air around Gavin's ear as it flashed by. Gavin lowered the Uzi and sent rounds through Scanlon's face, blowing shards of Scanlon's skull in all directions.

Across the grass the picnicking families were fleeing, their screams fading as they ran to the stand of pine trees two hundred yards away.

Gavin felt light headed and dry mouthed. He dropped the Uzi into the Trans Am, then got behind the wheel. He left Griffith Park, taking the scenic route past the zoo.

Gavin parked three blocks from Little Tokyo. He took off his sport coat and wrapped the reloaded Uzi in it. He tucked the bundle under his arm, then walked quickly to First Street.

He had no trouble finding the restaurant that he had been taken to earlier. From the outside, it looked like a Hollywood set, an art director's nightmare. A Shinto temple gateway, the lintel and crosspiece painted a dull white, framed a building that looked more like a mosque than a Japanese restaurant.

Gavin didn't know if Oki was inside or not. Gavin hoped that Oki was going to wait for Shigata to return, to make sure that everything went according to plan.

Or perhaps Oki had decided not to push his luck and had ducked out as soon as possible, taking the microcassette with him.

Gavin would soon find out.

He entered the restaurant quickly, brushing past the lovely hostess as he headed for the stairway to the second floor. He heard her exclamation behind him, but he didn't turn around. Gavin took the stairs two at a time, hurling his jacket to the floor, freeing the Uzi.

There was a corridor at the top of the stairs; Gavin wheeled to his right. A *yakuza* wearing a white shirt and gray trousers saw Gavin coming and shouted something as he hauled his revolver out of his waistband. But Gavin was already on him, ramming the Uzi's barrel into his gut, then following through with a clubbing action as the *yakuza* doubled over.

Gavin turned the doorknob and pushed open the door.

There were three men in the room and two already had their .44s in position. The third, Oki himself, stood by the room's rear door, which Gavin knew led down a flight of stairs to the alley.

Gavin hurled himself to the left as the .44s boomed, splintering the doorway above Gavin's head. Too much gun for the job, Gavin thought. They had trouble controlling the massive pieces.

Gavin's Uzi was spitting before he stopped moving—one burst ruptured their chests, blowing pink meat against the walls.

Oki was already out the door. Gavin raced to the stairway in time to see Oki running for the open back door of a Lincoln Continental.

Gavin fired a dozen rounds, the last one or two catching Oki low on the arm, spinning him around. A small object sailed from his hand, and as he stumbled near the open door a *yakuza* leaned out of the car and opened up on Gavin with an automatic rifle, driving him back into the room. Gavin heard the screech of tires, then the shouts and screams coming from the restaurant below.

Quickly, Gavin checked outside. The Lincoln was gone, but there, near the dumpster that served the restaurant, was the microcassette.

Gavin raced down the stairs, picked up the microcassette, and continued running till he was out of the alley and back on First Street.

Gavin took his time walking to his car, joining the other pedestrians who craned their necks as a dozen LAPD black-and-whites roared down First towards the Lotus Restaurant.

There was a gasp of shock from the receptionist at the Japan-America Trading Corporation when Mr. Oki limped into the outer office.

He had bruised his knee, wrenching it when he ran for the car. But what caused the outcry of shock was the sight of Oki's hand.

A round from the Uzi had shattered his wrist—the bone protruded, splintered and sharp. Blood drenched his suit, and the pallor of his face, his trembling, pained eyes, made the receptionist pick up the telephone and call for emergency medical aid.

Oki brushed past her and walked directly to his office. He slammed the door shut, then walked to his desk. His consciousness was dimming quickly, and he wanted to act while in this half-awake state. There was so little difference between being and nonbeing, he thought.

In the top drawer of his desk, underneath a manila-bound report, was a snub-nose .38, fully loaded. Oki gripped it, its weight tugging at his arm. Oki smiled. His humiliation was over.

He raised the .38 to his right temple and pulled the trigger. The round imploded his right temple, then bulged out the left side of his skull, splattering bone fragments, blood, and brain matter against the wall.

The office manager of the Japan-America Trading Corporation was the first person to enter Oki's office. He gave the office help—the secretaries and file clerks—the rest of the day off; most of the executives stayed on to offer whatever assistance possible to the authorities.

Before the day was out, the office manager had already received three requests, from junior executives in the corporation, for permission to relocate in Mr. Oki's corner office.

The view was incomparable.

eighteen

Gavin stopped at a diner off Interstate 5—heavy fog had made further driving too risky. He collected a dollar's worth of change from the cashier, then phoned the San Francisco Police Department. He wanted to talk to Inspector Cooke.

"So you're still alive," Cooke said when he got on the line. "I don't imagine you want to tell me where you're calling from?"

"You wouldn't want to know," Gavin said. "But I've got some news for you. First, I've got the microcassette that contains the plans for the encryption device. Contact NSA, because I'm turning it over to you."

"That will be a pleasure," Cooke answered.

"And watch out for a cop named Meehan. He's been in on this from the start. He's been leaking information to the kidnappers. He's going to suddenly come into some new evidence that lays the whole deal at the feet of the head of security at Electrotec—a guy named Scanlon. Scanlon's dead, but he was involved. The head of Electrotec, Clayton Edwards, is the brains behind the deal. See if you can catch up with him."

"I'll give it my best shot," Cooke answered.

"I'm heading back to San Francisco right now. I want to check on Duffy. I hope I won't be having any problems with you."

"If you've got that cassette, you don't have any problems with me."

"And tell NSA that I'm cooperating—I don't want them all over me when I get back to Colorado."

"Will do."

When Gavin returned to his booth the waitress had left his order of coffee and apple pie. He ate slowly, in no rush. There was little chance that Cooke was going to find Edwards. Edwards was gone as soon as the money was in his hands.

Gavin shook his head. Scanlon had been a real fool, thinking that he was going to double-cross Edwards at the last moment. Edwards was a coward, and that type is always too careful to be caught stupidly.

The diner was filling with fog-bound motorists, most of them in a glum mood. The thick fog on Interstate 5 north of Los Angeles was well known; freak pileups of ten to fifty cars were fairly commonplace when motorists tried to drive through the dense muck.

Gavin was in no rush. He was convinced that Edwards was gone, his escape route carefully laid out before the deal went down.

That only left Duffy, and rushing to San Francisco wasn't going to help him a bit.

Gavin had two more cups of coffee while the fog, instead of lifting, grew thicker. He took a room at the motel across the street, showered, then collapsed on the king-size bed. He hadn't realized how exhausted he was, and the utter comfort and quiet of his surroundings took over. He was asleep ten minutes later.

When Gavin parked at San Francisco Memorial Hospital it was almost noon. The day had dawned clear and cold; Gavin had taken his time on the drive.

There was a uniformed officer on duty outside Duffy's room—belated security always amused Gavin. "Can I help you?" The cop asked Gavin as he approached room 312.

"I'd like to see Duffy."

"No visitors allowed." The cop's eyes had narrowed. His hand rested lightly on his nightstick.

"Is Cooke available?"

"He's not here, if that's what you mean," the cop answered.

It took fifteen minutes to run Cooke to ground, and when he came on the line there was a cheery note in his voice. "Won't let you in, will he?" Cooke chuckled.

"Can you call him off?"

"I'll do better than that. Hang around for ten minutes. I'll be right over."

When Cooke arrived Gavin handed him the microcassette. Cooke hefted the small object in his hand. "So this is what it was all about."

Cooke eyed Gavin. "I called NSA this morning. They don't like it, but they'll go along with it."

"Sweet guys."

"They wanted to lean on you, cassette or not. The way they look at it, you need investigating."

"The way they look at it, everyone needs investigating."

Cooke smiled. "Yeah." He slipped the cassettte in his suit pocket. "C'mon. Let's see your friend."

They entered room 312. Duffy was sitting up in bed, his head still bandaged. There were dark ugly circles around each eye. "What the hell are you doing here?" Duffy asked when he saw Gavin.

"I thought you two were friends," Cooke said.

"We are," Gavin said. A slow smile crossed Duffy's round face.

"The doc says you're going to be as good as new in a few weeks," Cooke said to Duffy.

"I was never new," Duffy said. A frown etched lines in his forehead. "I can't get any information around here. The last thing I remember was going into Susan's apartment, and a fight. What happened? How is she?"

Cooke looked at Gavin.

"She's dead," Gavin said.

Duffy's face drained of color. "Dead? Why? How?"

Gavin shook his head. "She got caught in the middle of something ugly. We tried to bring her back, but it didn't work. They killed her before we could get to her."

Duffy made a fist. "I wish to hell I was out of this hospital," he said slowly. "And soon I will be."

"You're right," Gavin said. "There's time enough to finish this business."

A storm front had moved in from the Pacific, dumping two inches of rain in Los Angeles, and a foot of snow in High Card, Colorado.

February was like that. It was the beginning of the feeling that winter would never end. Gavin hiked down Main Street towards Dorn's shop.

A sharp wind caught him; Gavin's facial muscles tightened against the raw chill. He tucked in his chin as he passed Kendall's Book Store.

She was inside, clad in a white ski sweater, her long blonde hair golden in the yellow interior light. She waved when she saw Gavin go by, and he waved back.

Tonight was the dinner party.

By the time he arrived at Dorn's he felt stiff with cold. Dorn grinned at him. "You think you'll ever get used to these winters?" he asked.

"What for?" Gavin answered. "I like being so cold that my teeth hurt. Doesn't everyone?"

Dorn filled a cup three-quarters full with thick black coffee, then floated a double shot of Bushmill's on top. "Drink," he said.

Gavin was grateful for the hot drink. He gripped the steaming mug in his hands, warming them, then lifted the mug to his lips.

The phone rang.

"For you," Dorn said. He looked concerned. Gavin never received phone calls at Dorn's except from the few locals who had business with him. The person on the other end of the line was not local.

It was Duffy. Dorn prepared a hot drink

for himself, listening to Gavin's conversation. Duffy was up and about, had been back on the job for a month.

Everything was fine. Between Cooke and Duffy, they had been able to short-circuit any interest that NSA had in Bob Evans of High Card, Colorado.

Duffy had even more news than that. Clayton Edwards had surfaced. He had been reported living in a refurbished hacienda near the provincial capital of Concepción, Paraguay.

Edwards had worn out his welcome, but his money was still a powerful force. The local authorities in Concepción had been alerted to Edward's presence, and they in turn had contacted an American consular official, who paid Edwards a personal call. Edwards had agreed to leave Paraguay, and was reported preparing to cross the border into Brazil, across the Apa River.

Once in Brazil, he would be lost for good—that country was too large and too primitive, in the western portion, for Edwards ever to be located again.

Gavin had told Duffy to cheer up. It wasn't a lost cause yet. When he hung up he turned to Dorn. "How about another of those special coffees?"

That night the dinner party at Kendall's was a rousing success. Gavin had been charming, and Kendall was pleased. It was the first time that Gavin had met any members of Kendall's family. Her brother had driven down from Denver, bringing their mother with him. It was a ritual meal, a preliminary to entry into the Kendall Family.

After dinner Gavin said good-night at the front door. "I'll be out of town for a few days," he said to Kendall.

She frowned. "Really? On business?" Her face was a cold mask.

"Sort of," Gavin said. "Unfinished business."

"I thought you told me that you were finished with all of that. You just wanted to settle down."

"See you in a few days."

A closed door was his answer.

Clayton Edwards pushed back from the formal dining table, picked up the small silver bell, and rang. A young woman, her long black hair braided, entered the room and began clearing the dinnerware.

She returned a few moments later with a demitasse of espresso. Clayton Edwards nodded to her absently, lighting a long thin cigar, watching her as she left the room.

It was very quiet.

It had been a pleasant few months in Paraguay, but in a way he was glad that he was moving. He was a new hand at this kind of living, and his first choice—a remote section in the interior of a landlocked country—had proved to be inconvenient.

Besides, the local authorities were not as malleable as he would have supposed. They had warned him of his behavior, and when the child died, they had returned and told him that they had notified the American consulate.

There was no proof that he had had anything to do with the child's death. Had there been, Clayton Edwards was certain that they would have arrested him.

That was not good enough. He couldn't afford to live in a place where his money couldn't cover him. He had heard that across the river, in western Brazil, there was still plenty of room for a man who knew what he wanted out of life—no questions asked.

The peasants in the village had become a problem as well. He could understand the parents of the dead child—they would be eager to seek revenge.

But Clayton Edwards had been surprised when so many of the villagers joined in. Edwards had been forced to travel to Asunción, Paraguay's capital, and there recruit a trio of bodyguards, brutal cold-blooded men who knew how to treat malcontents.

Since their arrival, his hacienda had been left in peace.

The move would require a trip to some

commercial center in Brazil, where he could notify the bank in Switzerland of his new home. A day at the most, and his business would be done.

He arose from the table and crossed the room to the small wall safe. He twisted the dial quickly, eager to feel the security that his money gave him.

He had fifty thousand dollars on hand, more than enough to cover expenses for two years in the remote outposts he was attracted to.

Edwards took out the small leather case and placed it on the table. He sipped his espresso, a smile on his lips. He opened the leather case and thumbed through the crisp, familiar bills.

The burst of automatic fire froze his hand. Quickly Edwards moved to the safe, reached in, and withdrew a .45 automatic. "Luis!" he called out.

There was no answer.

Edwards heard the sound of men running. Then there was another burst of automatic fire.

Then it was quiet.

He heard footsteps. "Edwards?" The voice was soft, vaguely familiar. He thumbed the safety on the automatic. His throat was dry, his eyes wide with apprehension.

He heard a sound behind him and whirled,

pulling the trigger on the .45 in a reflex action, blowing a chunk of wall away.

Edwards saw him then. He was standing outside the French doors, his weapon pointed at Edwards. As if in a dream, Clayton Edwards dragged the .45 around, conscious of his slowness. He felt the impact simultaneously with the muzzle flash, his flesh tearing, a fresh wetness all around him. As he lay on the floor in the sudden warmth of his own blood he watched as the gray-eyed man entered the room. The pain was sudden when it came, a hot, thrusting snake in his gut. Clayton Edwards gasped and tried to swallow, but his throat wasn't working.

The gray-eyed man stuffed the leather case in his backpack, then turned and walked towards the French doors. Clayton Edwards was on his belly, crawling, leaving a snail's trail of red gristle.

He could barely breath. "Who are you?" Edwards gasped, the room dimming suddenly. "Why are you doing this?"

But the gray-eyed man was already gone.